"Why are you doing this?" Sadie asked, and could have kicked herself.

Did it really matter why? Having his mouth just a breath from hers, having his gaze locked on her, was something she'd thought about for years, and now that it was happening she questioned it? What was wrong with her?

"Am I making you nervous?" Ethan asked in response.

"If you were?"

"Then I'd stop."

"Then I'm not nervous."

"Glad to hear it." Suddenly any trace of humor was gone from his eyes. His features were taut as he stared at her as if seeing her for the first time.

* * *

Bombshell for the Boss by Maureen Child is part of Harlequin Desire's #1 bestselling series, Billionaires and Babies: Powerful men...wrapped around their babies' little fingers.

Dear Reader,

Chocolate. Oh, yes. What could be better than a rich, sexy hero who owns a chocolate empire? A dream come true, right?

In *Bombshell for the Boss*, you'll meet Ethan Hart, CEO of Heart Chocolate. He's got it all and his life is in perfect order, just the way he likes it. And then... the bombshell.

A decades-old promise to a friend comes back to haunt him when he becomes the legal guardian to a six-month-old girl.

Sadie Matthews is Ethan's executive assistant. She's been in love with him for five years and knows it's going nowhere. She decides to quit and find a new life, but changes her mind when Ethan offers her a small fortune to stay and help him with that baby.

Meanwhile, Ethan's brother, Gabriel, is causing trouble and his girlfriend, Pam, is egging him on. Suddenly the Hart family is in turmoil and Ethan finds that the only stable thing in his life is Sadie, the woman who wants to leave him.

Together, they have to build something new—if they can.

I hope you enjoy Ethan and Sadie's story. I had a good time with them. Please visit me on Facebook and let me know what you think!

Until next time, happy reading!

Maureen

MAUREEN CHILD

———

BOMBSHELL FOR THE BOSS

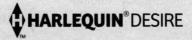

Recycling programs
for this product may
not exist in your area.

ISBN-13: 978-1-335-60338-8

Bombshell for the Boss

Copyright © 2018 by Maureen Child

Printed in U.S.A.

Maureen Child writes for the Harlequin Desire line and can't imagine a better job. A seven-time finalist for a prestigious Romance Writers of America RITA® Award, Maureen is the author of more than one hundred romance novels. Her books regularly appear on bestseller lists and have won several awards, including a Prism Award, a National Readers' Choice Award, a Colorado Romance Writers Award of Excellence and a Golden Quill Award. She is a native Californian but has recently moved to the mountains of Utah.

Books by Maureen Child

Harlequin Desire

Visit her Author Profile page at Harlequin.com, or maureenchild.com, for more titles.

One

"We already talked about this." Ethan Hart leaned back and stared across the desk at his younger brother. Elbows propped on the arms of his chair, Ethan steepled his fingers and narrowed his gaze. Irritation simmered inside him. How often did they have to go through this? Not for the first time, Ethan wondered if having his little brother on the board was a good idea.

Gabriel Hart pushed up from the visitor's chair and shoved both hands into his slacks pockets. "No, Ethan. *We* didn't discuss anything. *You* commanded."

One eyebrow winged up as Ethan lifted his gaze to meet Gabe's. "Since you remember our last conversation so well, I wonder why you're here trying to go over it all again."

"Because even as stubborn as you are, Ethan, I keep hoping that I'll manage to get through to you."

"I'm stubborn?" Ethan laughed and shook his head. "That's funny, coming from you."

"Damn it, I'm trying to do something important," Gabe argued. "Not just for me, but for the company."

And he believed that, Ethan knew. Gabriel had always been the one to try new things, to push envelopes. Well, that was no problem for himself. But for this company? Trying something new wasn't worth risking a reputation it had taken generations to build.

This was an old argument, getting older by the second. Ever since Gabe had taken his place in the Hart family chocolate company, the brothers had been doing battle. Ethan regretted that, because he and his younger brother had always been close. But the bottom line was Ethan was in charge and it was Ethan who would make the final call about the direction their company would take. And Gabriel was just going to have to find a way to live with that.

Standing up, he faced his brother. "Reality is, Gabe, we sold thirty-one *million* pounds of chocolate last year. The company is doing fine. We don't need to take risks."

"Damn it, Ethan, taking risks is how our great-grandfather started this company in the first place."

"True. Joshua Hart started the business," Ethan said tightly. "And each generation has kept our reputation a sterling one. We're one of the top five chocolate companies in the world. Why in the hell would I want to take risks now?"

"To be number *one*," Gabriel snapped. Clearly frustrated, he shoved a hand through his black hair. "Times change, Ethan. Tastes change. We can keep making the same great chocolate *and* we can add to our lists. Bring in new tastes and textures. Attract different customers, younger customers who'll stick with us for decades."

Ethan looked at his brother and felt twin tugs of affection and irritation. It had always been like this between them. Ethan had been looking out for his younger brother most of their lives. Gabriel was the wild one. The one who wanted to try new things, see new places. He was a risk taker and Ethan had rescued him from more than one escapade over the years. And that was fine, Ethan supposed, until it came to business. There, Ethan wasn't going to buck traditions that had built his family company into a worldwide giant.

"You want to start your own company," Ethan said softly, "and sell oregano chocolate or whatever, help yourself. Heart Chocolates will remain at the top of its game by giving our customers exactly what they want and expect from us."

"Very safe," Gabriel muttered, shaking his head. "And boring."

Ethan snorted. "Success is *boring*? We do what works, Gabe. We always have."

Gabe slapped both hands down on Ethan's desk and leaned in. "I'm a part of this company, Ethan. We're brothers. This is *our* family business. Dad left it to both of us. And I want a say in how it runs."

"You get a say," Ethan said, as irritation simmered even hotter, becoming a ball of anger in the pit of his stomach.

"And you get the final vote."

"Damn straight I do. The company was left to both of us, but I'm in charge." Ethan met his brother's gaze and tried to ease the hot knot of fury that settled inside him. He understood what was driving Gabriel. His younger brother wanted to make his mark on the family company. But that didn't mean Ethan was going to gamble everything they'd built on his brother's risky ideas.

Yes. They could introduce new flavors, new types of chocolates with strange fillings and flavors that bucked every traditional norm. But their current customers wouldn't be interested—they knew what they wanted and counted on Heart Chocolates to provide it.

"Never let me forget that, do you?" Gabriel pushed off the desk, then stuffed his hands into his pockets.

"Look, Gabe, I get what you're trying to do, but it's my responsibility to protect the reputation we've spent generations building."

"You think I'm trying to wreck it?" Gabe stared at him, astonished.

"No. You're just not considering all the angles of this idea." Ethan's patience was so strained now he felt as if he were holding on to the last remaining threads of a rope from which he was dangling over the edge of a cliff. So he tried a different tactic. "Introducing a new line of chocolates, hoping to reel in new customers, would require a huge publicity campaign well beyond what we already have in place."

"Pam says the campaign could be run within the plan that we're already using."

One of Ethan's eyebrows lifted. "Pam, huh? Who's she?"

Gabriel took a deep breath and looked as though he regretted letting that name slip. "Pam Cassini," he said. "She's smart as hell. She's setting up her own PR firm and she's got some great ideas."

"And you're sleeping with her," Ethan added for him. Did this explain Gabriel's latest attempt to change things up? Was his new girlfriend behind it all?

"What's that got to do with anything?"

Before he could answer, Ethan heard a brisk knock on the door, then it swung open and his assistant, Sadie Matthews, poked her head inside. Her big blue eyes shifted from him to Gabe and back again before she asked, "War over?"

"Not even close," Gabriel said.

Ethan scowled at him. "What is it, Sadie?"

"The shouts are starting to drift out onto the

floor," she said, stepping into the room and closing the door behind her.

For just a second, Ethan took a long, hard look at her.

Sadie had been his executive assistant for five years. Tall, she had short, curly blond hair, dark blue eyes and it seemed to him that a smile was always tugging at her mouth. She was efficient, beautiful, smart, sexy, and completely off-limits. Over the years, he'd actually had to train himself to not react to her as he would if she didn't work for him. It wasn't easy. Hell, one look at her curves would bring any red-blooded man to his knees.

Her mouth was a temptation and that spark of barely restrained rebellion in her eyes had always intrigued him. Early on, he'd even considered firing her just so he could try for a taste. But she was too damn good at her job.

Walking toward his desk, she said, "I actually heard a couple people placing bets on which one of you would win this round."

"Who?" Ethan demanded with another hard look at his brother.

She looked surprised at the question and shook her head. "I'm not going to tell you."

"What the hell, Sadie…"

She ignored him and looked at Gabriel. "The new distributor is waiting in your office for that meeting you have scheduled. If you'd rather, I could tell him you're in a heated battle with your brother…"

Gabriel gritted his teeth, but nodded. "Fine. I'll go." He looked at his brother. "But this isn't over, Ethan."

"Never thought it was," he said with a sigh.

When Gabriel was gone, Ethan asked, "Did you bet on me?"

She grinned. "How do you know I placed a bet?"

"You're too smart *not* to bet on me."

"Wow, a compliment for me and a pat on your own back all at the same time. Impressive."

"Is the distributor really in Gabe's office or did you do that just to break up the war?"

"Oh, he's really there," she said, walking toward the bank of windows. "But I did want to break up the argument, so I would have made something up if I'd had to."

"He's driving me crazy." Ethan turned and moved to stand beside her at the windows overlooking the Pacific Ocean. January could be cold and gray in Southern California, but winter seas had their own magic. The water was as dark as the sky, with waves rolling relentlessly toward shore. Surfers posed on their boards, waiting for the perfect wave, and a few boats with brightly colored sails skimmed the water's surface. The scene should have calmed him—it usually did. But this thing with Gabriel was getting more irritating every time it came up.

"He still wants to make some changes to the chocolate line, doesn't he."

Ethan glanced at Sadie. "And now he's got some woman helping him wage his campaign."

"It's not a completely crazy idea," she said with a shrug.

He stared at her. "Not you, too."

Sadie shrugged again. "Change isn't always a bad thing, Ethan."

"In my experience, it is," he argued. He took her shoulders, ignored the leap of heat inside, then turned her to face him. Once she was, he released her and stepped back before saying, "People always talk about changing their lives. New car, new house, new hair color, hell, new beliefs. Well, there's something to be said for stasis. For finding what works and sticking with it."

"Okay, but sometimes change is the only route left open to you."

"Not this time," he muttered. Turning his back on her and the view, he headed to his desk, sat down and reached for the latest marketing report. He gave her a quick glance. "Sadie, if you're going to side with Gabriel on this, I don't want to hear it. I'm not in the mood to have another argument for change."

"Right. Well, we all have to do things we don't want to do."

"What?" He looked up at her.

She blew out a breath and handed him a single sheet of paper. "I'm quitting my job."

"You can't quit. We have a meeting in twenty minutes."

"And yet…"

Ethan just stared at her, not really sure he'd heard her correctly. This was coming out of the blue and made absolutely no sense. "No, you're not."

She waved the paper. "Read the letter, Ethan."

He snatched it from her and skimmed the neatly typed lines. "This is ridiculous." He held it out to her. "I'm not accepting this."

Sadie put her hands behind her back so she wouldn't be at all tempted to take the letter and pretend none of this had happened. Oh, she had known quitting was going to be hard. Had known that Ethan would fight her on this, and she was a little worried he might convince her to stay. Because she didn't really want to leave Heart Chocolates.

But, she reminded herself, she really didn't want to spend the next five years of her life as she'd spent the previous five. Hopelessly in love with a boss who saw her as nothing more than an efficient piece of office furniture.

"You can't quit," he argued. When she refused to take back her letter of resignation, he tossed it face-down onto his desk, as if he couldn't bring himself to even see it again. "We've got the spring campaign to finalize, the rehab at the factory—"

"And all of it will get done without me," Sadie said, and hoped he didn't hear the nearly wistful tone in her voice.

"Why?" he demanded, scowling at her. "Is this about a raise? Fine. You have it."

"It's not about money, Ethan," she said tightly. She already made more money than she would at any other job. Ethan was generous with his employees. That wasn't the issue at all.

He stood up. "All right, an extra two weeks of vacation a year, *plus* the raise."

She laughed at the idea and suddenly relaxed her guard. Really, for being such a good boss, he was also completely clueless sometimes. "Ethan, I don't take my vacation *now*. What good is two more weeks to me?"

"You're being unreasonable."

"I'm being pragmatic."

"I disagree."

"I'm sorry about that," she said, and she really was. Sadie didn't *want* to leave. Didn't *want* to never see him again. In fact, that thought opened up a dark, empty pit in the bottom of her stomach. Which told her she simply had no other choice.

"Then what's this about?"

"I want a life," she said, and hated how desperate those four words sounded.

But she'd spent the last eight years of her life working for *Heart* chocolates, the last five of which she'd been Ethan's assistant. She worked outrageous hours, hardly ever saw her family, and the houseplants in the condo she'd purchased the year before were dried-out sticks because she was never there often enough to water them.

She wanted romance. Sex. Maybe a family of her own before she was too old to get any of that.

"You have a life," he said, clearly affronted at the accusation that he'd somehow cheated her. "You're integral to this business. To *me*."

If only.

The real problem here was that she'd been in love with Ethan for years now. It was empty, completely one-sided and guaranteed to leave her a bitter old woman one day. Nope. For her own sake, she had to quit.

Shaking her head, she said, "That's work, Ethan, and there's more to life than work."

"Not that I've noticed," he complained.

"That's part of the problem," she argued. "Don't you get it? We work hideously long hours, come in on weekends, and last year you even called me in from my cousin's wedding to help you cover that mix-up with the Mother's Day shipment."

"It was important," he reminded her.

"So was Megan's wedding," she told him, shaking her head. "No, I have to do this. It's time for a change."

"Change again," he muttered, standing up and coming around the desk to stop right in front of her. "I'm really getting sick of that word."

"Change isn't always bad."

"Or good," he pointed out. "When things are working, why screw it up?"

"I knew you'd hate this and maybe it was bad timing coming in to talk to you right after your latest battle with Gabe. But yes. I need a change." She stared up into his grass-green eyes and felt a pang of regret that she was leaving. His dark brown hair was mussed, no doubt because he'd been stabbing his fingers through it again while arguing with Gabe. His tie was loosened and that alone was so damn sexy, her breath caught in her throat.

What was it about this man that hit her on so many levels? It wasn't just how gorgeous he was or the way he made her yearn with just a glance. He was strong and smart and tough and the combination was a constant temptation to her. So resigning was really her only choice.

How could she want him so badly and stay in a position that guaranteed she'd never have him?

"Damn it, Sadie what is it you want changed, exactly?"

"My *life*," she said, looking up into his eyes and willing him to see *her*, not just his always professional assistant. But he never would. She was like the fax machine or a new computer. There to do a job. "Do you know my brother, Mike, and his wife, Gina, just had their *third* baby?"

Confusion shone in his eyes. "So? What's that got to do with you?"

"Mike's wife is two years younger than me." She threw her hands up in disgust. "She has three kids. I have four dead plants."

"What the hell does *that* mean?"

She sighed a little. She'd known going in that quitting wouldn't be easy. That Ethan would try to keep her by offering raises, promotions, vacations. But she hadn't realized how hard it would be to tell him what was bothering her. What was driving her to leave. Heck, she'd only recently figured it out for herself.

"I want a family, Ethan. I want a man to love me..." *You*, her brain whispered, but she shut that inner voice down fast. "I want kids, Ethan. I'm almost thirty."

"Seriously?" He pushed the edges of his jacket back and stuffed both hands into his pants pockets. "That's what this is about? A biological clock moment?"

"Not just a moment," she told him. "I've been thinking about this for a while. Ethan, we work fifteen-hour days, sometimes more. I haven't been on a date in forever and haven't had *sex* in three *years*."

He blinked.

She winced. Okay, she hadn't meant to tell him that. Bad enough that *Sadie* knew the pitiful truth. Downright embarrassing for Ethan to know it. "My point is, I don't want to look back when I'm old and gray and all alone—except for a cat and I don't even like cats—and have the only thing I can say about my life be, *Boy, I really was a good assistant. Kept that office running smoothly, didn't I?*"

"Doesn't sound like a bad thing."

Exasperated, Sadie stabbed her index finger at him. "That's because *you* don't have a life, either." Yes, it had been forever since she'd been with anyone. But he was no better. "You bury yourself in your work. You never talk to anyone but me or Gabe. You own a damn mansion in Dana Point, but you're never there. You eat takeout at your desk and pour everything you have into charts and ledgers, and that's not healthy."

One dark eyebrow arched. "Thanks very much."

Sadie took a step back, mostly because standing so close to him was hard on her nerve endings. He smelled good. His jaw was tight, his eyes flashing and he looked...too tempting. Not for the first time, she wondered what would happen if she threw herself at his chest and wrapped her arms around his neck. Would he hold her back? Kiss her senseless?

Or would he be horrified and toss her to one side?

Since she was quitting, she could easily find out the answers. But the truth was, she wasn't sure she wanted to know. Sometimes a really good fantasy was way better than reality.

"This isn't about me and my life," he pointed out.

"In a way it is," she said. "Maybe if you hire an assistant who insists on a nine-to-five schedule, you'll get out of this office once in a while."

"Fine." He jumped on her statement. "You want nine to five, we can do that."

Sadie laughed. "No, we can't. Remember Megan's wedding?" Her cousin had been hurt that Sadie had slipped out of the chapel and missed the whole thing. And Sadie hadn't liked it, either. "I'm really sorry, Ethan, but I have to quit. I'll stay for two weeks, train a replacement."

"Who?" He crossed his arms over his chest and dared her with his eyes to come up with a suitable replacement.

"Vicki in Marketing."

"You're kidding."

"What's wrong with her?"

"She *hums*. Constantly."

Okay, she had to give him that one. He wasn't the only one to complain about Vicki. Worse, Sadie was pretty sure the woman was tone deaf. "Fine. Beth in Payroll."

"No." He shook his head. "Her perfume is an assault on the senses."

Typical, she thought. Of course he would find something wrong with everyone she suggested. He might be young, gorgeous and a sex-on-a-stick walking fantasy, but he had the resistance to change of a ninety-year-old.

Good thing she'd been prepared for this. "How about Rick? He's been working here for two years. He knows the business."

If anything, his jaw got tighter. "Rick agrees with Gabriel. I'm not going to spend every day arguing with my assistant."

True. So it came down to this. To *him* suggesting her replacement. "Who do you suggest, then?"

"You." He was frowning and somehow that only made him look sexier.

What was *wrong* with her?

"We're a team, Sadie. A good one. Why break that up?"

Though she loved the fact that he didn't want her to leave, she knew she had to go for her own peace of mind. How could she ever look for love somewhere else when she was too wrapped up in Ethan Hart? God, how pitiful did that sound?

"I'll find someone," she said firmly.

He didn't look happy at that, but he jerked a nod. "And you agree not to leave until a replacement is trained."

She narrowed her eyes on him, because she saw the trap. If he never agreed to a replacement, she'd never get that person trained and thus, never leave. "And you agree to accept the replacement."

He shrugged. "If this nameless person can do the job, of course."

"You sound so reasonable." Sadie tipped her head to one side and watched him closely. "Why don't I believe you?"

"Suspicious nature?"

His eyes flashed and her insides skittered in response. Seriously, from the moment she'd taken this job with Ethan Hart, Sadie had been half in love with him. And over the years, she'd taken the full-on tumble. She still wasn't sure why. Ethan wasn't anywhere near her ideal man.

She'd put a lot of time and thought into what she wanted. Yes, Ethan was gorgeous. Really way *too* handsome. Women were always tripping over themselves trying to get close to him. Yes, he was successful, but he was driven by his work to the exclusion of everything else in his life. She didn't know if he liked children because he was never around any. She didn't know if he was an amazing lover—though she'd had quite a few dreams in which he was the ultimate sex god. He had a sense of humor but he didn't use it often, and he was entirely too spoiled. Too used to getting his own way.

No, Ethan Hart was not the man for her and if she ever hoped to find that elusive lover, then she had to leave this job.

"I have reason to be suspicious," she said.

"Why would I lie?" he asked, feigning astonishment at the very idea.

"To get what you want."

"You know me so well, Sadie," he said, shaking his head. "Just one more reason why we make a good team."

They really did. Damn it. She hated having to leave and couldn't stand staying.

"Ethan, I'm serious," she said, lifting her chin and meeting his gaze squarely. "I'm quitting."

He looked at her for a long, silent minute. "Fine."

Just like that, his walls went up and his eyes went blank. "Wow, you're good at that."

"What?"

"Going from hot to cold in a blink."

"I don't know what you're talking about."

"Of course you do," Sadie said, staring into those beautiful eyes of his. "It's your signature move. Whenever a conversation or a negotiation starts going in a direction you don't approve of, up come the defenses. And now that I've officially resigned, I can tell you that I don't like it when you do it."

He frowned. "Is that right?"

"Yes." Sadie planted both hands on her hips. "You know, it's pretty great being able to just say what I'm thinking."

"I've never known you not to," he pointed out.

"Oh," she said with a laugh, "you have *no* idea the restraint I've shown over the years. Well, until now."

Those grass-green eyes narrowed on her. "Feeling pretty sure of yourself now, are you?"

"I'm always sure of myself, I just don't usually tell you everything I'm thinking. I have to admit," she added, "this is very freeing." Sure, she'd miss her job. And she'd *really* miss Ethan. But this was the best thing for her, and since she had to leave anyway, she was going to allow herself to enjoy her last two weeks with him. She'd be completely honest and hold nothing back. *Well, she wasn't about to admit she loved him or anything, but other than that...* "Also, I hate your coffee."

Now he looked insulted. "That's the world's finest Sumatra blend. I have a supply flown in every two months."

"Yes, and it's awful. It tastes like the finest Sumatran dirt."

"I don't think I care for this new blunt honesty policy."

Sadie grinned. She'd surprised him, something that was nearly impossible to do because Ethan Hart was always thinking two or three steps ahead of everyone else in the world. "Well, I think I like it."

"I could just fire you and be done with it," he warned.

"Oh, we both know you won't do that. You don't like change, remember?" She shook her head. If nothing else, she was completely confident in saying, "Never going to happen."

When a knock at the door sounded, they both turned and Ethan ordered, "Come in."

She was going to miss that bark of command.

"Mr. Hart? Ethan Hart?" A woman walked into the room carrying a baby that looked about six months old.

Instantly, Sadie's heart melted. The tiny girl was beautiful, with big brown eyes and wispy, black hair. She was chewing on her fist as the woman holding her crossed the room.

"Yes, I'm Ethan Hart. And you are?" The icy king-of-the-universe tone was back in his voice.

"Melissa Gable." She swung a black diaper bag off her shoulder and dropped it onto the visitor's chair. Digging into it one-handed, she came up with a manila envelope and handed it to Ethan. "I'm from Child Services. I'm here to deliver Emma Baker to you."

"Who's Emma Baker?" he asked warily.

"She is." And Ms. Gable handed the baby to Ethan.

Two

Not too long after his argument with Ethan, Gabriel was at his girlfriend Pam Cassini's house and his frustration felt as if it had a life of its own.

After the futile meeting with his brother, he'd hated walking back to his office, knowing everyone there had heard the argument and had known he'd lost. Gabe hated that Ethan wouldn't listen to reason and he hated having been born second. If Gabe had been the older brother, things at Heart Chocolates would be done differently.

"Instead," he mumbled, "I'll always be the little brother."

The junior partner, forced to fight for every scrap of recognition. Maybe he should have just gone home to the penthouse apartment he kept in Huntington Beach. He rented out half the top floor of the best hotel in the city and enjoyed the views and the convenience of twenty-four-hour room service and housekeeping.

Today he was in a foul mood, so he should have gone off by himself. But he didn't want to be alone, either.

"Oh hell, just admit it. You wanted to see Pam. Talk to her."

In the last six months, Pam Cassini had become more important to him than Gabriel was comfortable admitting. He hadn't been looking for any long-term relationship when he met her. And maybe that's why he'd fallen into one. He was no stranger to women wanting to hook up with one of the Hart brothers. But Pam was different. She was strong and smart and ambitious. She had her own career and she was as passionate about it as he was about his. He admired that.

Pam's tiny condo on a quiet street in Seal Beach was warm, welcoming, even to its bright yellow door flanked by terra-cotta pots filled with cheerful splashes of pink and white flowers. You could fit the whole damn place inside his apartment twice over, but there was something here his own place lacked. Pam.

He knocked and stalked the small porch while he waited. When she opened the door, Gabe blurted out, "My brother has a head like concrete."

Pam sighed, gave him a sympathetic look and opened the door wider. As Gabriel stomped past her, she asked, "He's still not willing to try a new line?"

He walked right into the living room and stopped in front of her small, white-brick gas fireplace, hissing with a few flames dancing over artificial logs. "He reacted like a vampire to garlic."

Shaking his head, Gabe turned around to face her in the narrow living room. He hardly noticed the comfortable furniture or the fresh coffee scenting the air. But as she walked toward him, even his fury with Ethan couldn't keep him from taking a moment to simply enjoy the view of *her.*

Pam was short, with a lush and curvy body that drove Gabe mad with hunger. Today she wore a tight, white T-shirt that clung to her breasts, and a pair of black yoga pants that defined every line of her butt, hips and legs. Her feet were bare and her toes were painted a deep scarlet.

She also had long black hair, the warmest brown eyes he'd ever seen and a wide, full mouth that had tempted him from the moment he first met her, more than six months ago. That was at a chocolate convention. He'd been there representing Heart Chocolates, of course, and Pam was handing out cards for her burgeoning PR business.

They'd had dinner that night, and by the end of the week they were inseparable. They'd been together ever since. In that short amount of time, Pam had become a kind of touchstone to him. She listened to his plans, liked his ideas and encouraged him to stand up to Ethan and fight for his own plans and ambitions. For all the good it was doing him.

She put one hand on his arm and looked up at him. "Trying to convince Ethan to change his mind isn't working. I told you, Gabe, all we really need is the chocolate recipe."

She'd been saying that for weeks now, and still Gabe hesitated. A chocolate recipe was sacred to a chocolatier. As ridiculous as it sounded, there actually were corporate spies out there, eager to steal a competitor's recipe. They could use it themselves, sell it, post it online or simply find a way to ruin it.

The Hart family had guarded their basic recipe for generations, just like every other chocolatier. And Gabe was hesitant to be the first member of the Hart family to trust an outsider with it.

"Think about it, Gabe," Pam was saying. "I know a great chocolate chef we can trust. With the recipe, we can have my guy make up samples of the new flavors and present them to Ethan as a done deal. Once he's tasted them, he'll see you're right and he'll jump on board."

A nice fantasy, Gabriel conceded, but hardly based in reality. He snorted. "You don't know Ethan."

"But I know you," she said softly, her voice dropping to the deep, breathless, sultry tone that always drove him crazy. "You're determined and when you believe in something, you just never quit. You don't give up, Gabe. You get what you go after. You got me, didn't you?"

In spite of everything, he smiled. How could he not, with this gorgeous woman looking up at him with hunger in her eyes? "We got each other."

"Ooh, good answer." Pam licked her lips, gave him a slow smile as she wrapped her arms around his neck and laid that luscious mouth over his. He went hard as stone instantly and gave himself up to the need she quickened inside him. He'd never known a fire like he felt with her. And a part of him wondered just how long that fire could last.

Then he stopped thinking entirely. Frustration, anger, everything else in the world simply faded away at the touch of her mouth to his. And as they moved together, in a rhythm that seared his blood and stole his breath, he knew there was nowhere else he wanted to be.

"Um," Sadie said, looking at the baby in Ethan's arms. "Is there anything you want to tell me?"

"It's not mine, if that's what you mean." He glared at her. He'd always been careful. He had no children and didn't plan on any. "I think I'd know if I'd made a baby. Besides, you just told me I don't have a life. How could it be mine?"

Sadie sighed. "First, not an 'it'. It's a girl."

"Fine. *She's* not mine."

"She is now," Sadie reminded him. Glancing through the paperwork the social worker had left behind, she said, "Bill and Maggie Baker were her parents. Ring a bell?"

He frowned and then frowned deeper when the baby kicked impossibly small legs, screwed up her face and let out a howl a werewolf would have been proud of. "What's wrong with it?"

"Being called *it*, probably," Sadie muttered, and snatched the baby from him. Positioning her on one hip, Sadie bounced and swayed in place until the child stopped crying.

Ethan took a step back just for good measure. The damn social worker had done her job. She'd handed off the baby, a car seat and a diaper bag, then left so quickly he hadn't had time to argue about anything. But he was ready to now. He couldn't take care of a damn baby. The idea was ludicrous. Who would have made *him* a guardian? Ethan had never been around a baby. He didn't even own a dog.

Baker. Bill Baker. Why did that sound familiar?

Ethan glanced at Sadie and, in spite of the situation, felt a hot rush of heat jolt through his system and settle in his groin. He'd worked with this woman for five years and he'd been fighting his instincts about her for every second of that time. It hadn't gotten any easier.

Hell, there she was, holding an infant and he *still* burned for her. She smiled at the baby, then kissed her forehead, and Ethan's belly jumped. He wanted her badly, and now that she'd resigned, he could have finally made a move on her. But if he did that and then was able to coax her into not quitting her job, after all, there'd be nothing but complications. So no move. He gritted his teeth, hissed in a breath and wished to hell for a cold shower.

Deliberately pushing thoughts of hot, steamy, incredible sex out of his mind, he went back to "Baker. Why do I know that name?" Then it hit him. Ethan stared at the baby, then Sadie. "Hell. I did know him. In college. We were roommates, for God's sake." As more of the past rushed into his mind, Ethan cursed under his breath and slapped one hand down on his desk. "We made a deal. A stupid deal."

"Involving children, I'm guessing."

"Funny." He glared at her, noticed the child watching him through wide, watery eyes, and looked away quickly. What was that ribbon of panic? Nothing scared him. But one look at that child and he was ready to run for the hills. That realization was humiliating.

"Yes," he said tightly, as memories crowded his mind. "It did involve children, obviously. Bill didn't have family. He and Maggie were engaged and she had been a foster child herself, so no family there, either. He asked me to be legal guardian to his kids if anything ever happened to him."

"And you did it?" The surprise in Sadie's voice jabbed at him.

The fact that he now regretted what he'd done so long ago didn't come into it. Instead, he was insulted that Sadie was incredulous that he would offer to help a friend. Did she really think so little of him? And because he *was* regretting it, Ethan had to ask himself if she wasn't right. Irritating.

"He was my friend." Offended at her tone, and the insinuation, he snapped, "I was twenty. Of course I agreed." Looking back now, faced with the consequences of that promise, Ethan couldn't believe he'd agreed. But in his defense, he added, "I never thought anything would come of it. At that age, you pretty much think you're immortal, anyway. Hell, he's the same age I am. Who would expect him to die?"

"Certainly not him, I think," Sadie said, skimming the paperwork again. "They were on a road trip to Colorado. The car went off the road, hit a tree. The authorities believe Bill fell asleep driving. Bill and Maggie were killed instantly." She turned to look at the baby. "It's a miracle she didn't die, too."

"Miracle." He pulled in a breath and blew it out again. From where he was standing the baby's survival looked like a damn tragedy. She'd lost both her parents in a blink and now found herself with a stranger who didn't have the first clue what to do with her. "What the hell am I supposed to do now?"

Sadie gave him a quizzical look, as if she couldn't believe he'd even asked the question. "You raise her."

"You say that like it's so simple."

"Ethan," Sadie said patiently, "she doesn't have anyone else. She needs you."

Well, that didn't sound good. He didn't want to be needed. Hell, he'd gone out of his way all these years to *avoid* any kind of connection with anyone. Except for his all-too-brief marriage. But that had turned out to be an excellent life lesson. Ethan had learned that he sucked at being a husband. He simply wasn't the *hearth and home* kind of man.

"You just told me I don't have a life," Ethan argued fiercely. "How am I supposed to give her one?"

At his rising voice, the baby started whimpering and Sadie rocked her a little more firmly. "I guess you're going to have to make some changes, Ethan."

There was that word again. Change usually screwed everything up. He liked his life just the way it was. He worked hard to keep his life unencumbered, rolling along on an expected road. And now...change.

Shaking his head, he backed up farther, as if he could actually maneuver his way out of this. And even as he argued for it, Ethan knew he couldn't. Stupidly or not, he'd made a promise, and when he gave his word he damn well kept it. When the blind panic lifted enough that he could begin to think clearly again, he said, "I don't need a life. I need a nanny."

"Oh, Ethan."

"What else should I do?" he demanded. "Get *married*? No. A nanny is the answer. All I have to do is find the right person. Someone qualified—" He broke off, checked his watch. "We're supposed to be in a meeting on the Donatello acquisition right now."

"Yes, well, we can't be." She looked at the baby as if to remind him of the hell his life had suddenly become. "I can tell you that Richard Donatello hasn't changed his mind about selling out to you."

"He will," Ethan said. "You could take care of her while I handle business."

"No." Sadie shook her head firmly. "I'm not your babysitter, I'm your assistant. Plus, I just quit, remember?"

"I remember you gave two weeks' notice. So you're still on the payroll."

"As an assistant."

"So assist me!" That came out as a desperate shout and he hated it. So did the baby. She started howling again and Ethan winced.

"Shh, shh," Sadie whispered, bouncing the baby and patting her back. Firing Ethan a hard look, she said, "Cancel the meeting, Ethan."

Damn it. She was right. The meeting had to wait. Fine. Meeting canceled. Sadie quits. Baby arrives. *Change is not good*, he reminded himself. And sometimes you simply had no choice but to adjust. Still, he told himself as something occurred to him, that didn't mean he couldn't help himself out. At least, temporarily. Before he could think better of it, Ethan blurted out, "I'll pay you one hundred thousand dollars if you stay for an extra month."

"What?" Her eyes went wide and her jaw dropped.

Of course he'd surprised her. Hell, he'd surprised himself. "A hundred thousand dollars," he repeated, then added, "on the condition you help me with…" He waved one hand at the baby.

"Her name is Emma," Sadie said wryly.

"Good. You already know that, so you're ahead of the game." Nodding to himself at the brilliance of his solution, he demanded, "Well? What do you say?"

"I think you're crazy," Sadie said. "But yes, I'll stay for a month. Help you find a nanny."

"And help me take care of it until then."

"Her."

"Right. *Her.*" He reached for his phone, punched a couple buttons and waited for a second. "Kelly. Tell the team the meeting's postponed until tomorrow. Something's…" he looked at Sadie and the baby "…come up." Huge understatement.

When he hung up, he looked at Sadie and deliberately shoved his hands into his slacks pockets so he couldn't be forced to hold the baby again. "Call Alice at the house, tell her what's happened. Have her get a room ready for the kid—order whatever she needs and offer a big cash bonus for quick delivery and setup."

"Ethan—"

"You still work for me, Sadie. Get it done." Then he walked to his desk, sat down and started working. He avoided looking at Sadie again and told himself it was for the best. Hell, the baby wouldn't want to be held by him, anyway.

A few hours later, Sadie and Ethan, along with the baby, were at Target, staring at a wall of baby supplies.

"How does anyone know what to get?" he asked of no one in particular.

"Well, here I've got a little experience," Sadie admitted. "On those rare Sundays off, I've been shopping with Gina, my sister-in-law."

"You're elected as guide, then."

Sadie noticed that he looked completely out of place in the perpetually crowded store. In his elegantly cut suit, he would have been much more at home in his meeting, or in a five-star restaurant, or even just sitting in his sleek black convertible. But here in Target, Ethan Hart was enough out of the ordinary that every woman who passed him paused to stare. Of course, that happened everywhere. The man practically oozed sex and success.

But at the moment, he was devoting himself to staying as far away from the big red cart and the baby strapped into it as humanly possible. Sadie gritted her teeth. She'd promised to *help* him with the baby, not do everything herself. Not even for a hundred-thousand-dollar bonus. This was Ethan's chance to step outside the carefully built path he'd designed for himself, and Sadie wanted to see him do it. But now wasn't the time for that argument. Pretty soon, the baby would be hungry. Or wet again. Or tired. Sadie would rather avoid the inevitable meltdown that she'd witnessed with her infant nephew just a couple weeks ago.

"Okay," she said abruptly. "First, we need diapers."

"Right." Ethan instantly turned to the task at hand. "But what size? There's a million of them." He scanned the shelves, looking like a blind man trying to feel his way through a forest.

"You held her. How much do you think she weighs?"

He pushed one hand through his hair. "Twenty pounds?"

"Okay," she said. "Start there. I'll get some formula and bottles and...*everything*."

Yes, she'd been shopping with Gina, stocking up on baby supplies, but that was just adding a few things to an already well-stocked house. *This* was starting from scratch, and she was overwhelmed with deciding what Ethan might need to care for Emma. He was right—there were just too many *things*.

While the baby slapped her hands on the cart and Ethan stayed at the end of the aisle, reading the descriptions on every bag of diapers, Sadie loaded in whatever she thought might be useful. Toys, a stuffed bear that Emma grabbed hold of and refused to release, bottles, bibs, nipples, pacifiers… The cart was pretty much full when Ethan turned and dropped a single package of diapers on top of it.

"One?" she asked, stunned. "Really? You think one package will do it?"

"How the hell do I know? You're the expert here."

"Ooh," Sadie said with a grin. "That had to have been hard for you to say. Ethan Hart, the man who's never wrong and must be obeyed at all costs."

He scowled. "I don't remember you being this sarcastic over the last five years."

"That's because I muttered most of it," she admitted. "Get two more packages to start and that should hold us."

"For what? The apocalypse?" He stared at the cart. "She doesn't really need all of that, does she?"

The baby frowned, as if she understood what Ethan had said and disapproved. Sadie almost laughed, but she was afraid it might sound hysterical, so she swallowed it. Busy shoppers rushed past them as music pumped through the store speakers. "Do you really want to find out in the middle of the night that you need something and you don't have it?"

"Oh, hell no. Fine. We'll take it all." He started to walk away, but Sadie stopped him.

"She needs clothes, too, Ethan."

He goggled at her. "This is incredible. How do people do this?"

"Well, most people don't have to do an entire stock-up run all in one day…"

"Right." He looked over the aisles they had just been picking clean and said, "You know, the chocolate business makes billions, but turns out, that's just peanuts. The *real* money is in baby junk. How can someone who can't even talk possibly need so much stuff?"

She almost felt sorry for him. Almost. This was a huge disruption in the placid lake that was his life. But hey, sink or swim. "It's a mystery. Come on. Baby clothes."

He followed after her, grumbling under his breath, and Sadie looked into Emma's eyes and grinned. In the five years she'd worked for the man, Sadie had never seen Ethan completely out of his element. And it was sort of endearing. She didn't need another reason to be drawn to him, though, so she really tried to dismiss what she was feeling.

Then he did it to her again when he picked up baby pajamas and discarded the penguins in favor of the ones covered in teddy bears. When he caught her looking at him quizzically, he shrugged and tossed the jammies into the cart. Then, pointing at the baby now chewing fiercely on the stuffed bear's ear, he said simply, "She likes bears."

Sadie took a deep breath to still the jolt of her heartbeat. He didn't want the baby, but he was doing everything he could to make sure she was cared for. He didn't like change, but he was so far accepting a huge one in his life. He didn't belong in Target, but here he stood. And God knew he shouldn't look so damn sexy, but there it was. Even as she thought it, she spotted a woman staring at Ethan with open admiration.

Sadie told herself to get past it. Get over it. She was going to leave Ethan behind so she could find the right man for her. No matter how she felt about Ethan, no matter how her blood burned when she looked at him, going after him was a catastrophe waiting to happen.

He wasn't the man for her and trying to pretend otherwise was just setting herself up for a crash. So she busied herself by concentrating on the shopping and promising herself that one day, she'd be doing this for her own family.

The sad part of that dream was Ethan wouldn't be a part of it.

Sadie had been to Ethan's house before, bringing him papers or running one of the parties he threw for distributors, but today felt different. They weren't there for business and it sort of colored how she looked at the house itself.

It was Spanish-style and gigantic, even by mansion standards. The red tiled roof made the white walls seem even brighter than they normally would have. The grounds, from the sweeping lawns to the flower beds and climbing roses over the pergola in the backyard, were lovingly tended by a team of gardeners and the floor-to-ceiling windows glinted in the winter sunlight. Behind the house, she knew, was a sloping yard that ran down to the cliffs where waves beat a constant rhythm against the rocks.

The view was majestic and the house itself was breathtaking. Every room was huge, open and appealing in an earthy, masculine way. Brown leather furniture and burnished wood decorated every room and the dark red ceramic tiles in the halls were a dramatic statement. Sadie's favorite spot was the Spanish-style, enclosed courtyard. Three sides of the house surrounded an outdoor living area, complete with comfortable furniture, a bar and kitchen. Terra-cotta pots held a wide variety of plants and the area provided a wonderful view of the ocean.

Today, though, she really didn't have the time to luxuriate in the place itself. She had a cranky baby in the backseat and a ton of things to unload.

Ethan came around and opened her car door.

The baby chose that moment to scream her fury and Ethan winced. "How does she hit those notes?"

"It's a gift."

"Why don't you take her inside? I'll get the gardener and some of his guys to empty out the cars."

Huffing out a breath, Sadie accused, "You're just trying to avoid touching her, aren't you?"

"See why I hired you?" he countered. "You're smart."

"Right." This did not bode well for Ethan and Emma. If he avoided the baby every chance he got, he'd never adapt to the new situation. Yes, he'd paid Sadie a lot of money to hang around until he got things settled. But she was going to make sure that he did at least half the baby care.

She got the little girl out of the car seat, plopped her on one hip and headed for the front door. Ethan wasn't too far behind her, but when she opened the front door and walked inside, they all stopped dead.

Alice, Ethan's housekeeper, was standing in the entryway, arms folded across her abundant chest and a frown etched deeply into her features. Really, Alice defied stereotypical logic. Looking at her round body and bright blue eyes, most people would have guessed her to be as kind as Mrs. Claus. Nothing could be further from the truth. Sadie had never understood why Ethan kept such an unpleasant woman working for him. It probably helped that he was rarely at home and so wasn't exposed to her much.

Alice's eyes narrowed accusingly on the baby.

"I'm the housekeeper," she said flatly. "I don't take care of children."

"Fine," Ethan said, pushing Sadie farther inside so he could step past her.

"I mean it." Alice lifted her chins and sniffed. "I've got my routine and I won't have it upset by an infant."

Sadie had never really liked Alice. No surprise there, since the woman was cold and distant. On those rare occasions when Ethan was here, in his own house, Alice behaved like he was an interloper. Normally, she had the run of the mansion on the cliffs. She was alone here more often than not and Sadie had a feeling it was only Ethan's inherent hatred of change that had kept him from firing the woman.

"I said fine," Ethan repeated. "Fernando and some of his guys are bringing the baby's food and—" he waved a hand to indicate everything else they'd dragged along "—stuff to the kitchen. Did the furniture for her room show up?"

"It did," Alice said, her mouth flattening into a grim line of displeasure. "Those men tracked dirt all over my floors and made a racket for nearly an hour."

Ethan just looked at her. "So her room's ready."

"It is, just don't expect me to clean up after an infant."

Sadie took a breath and clamped her mouth shut to avoid telling Alice exactly what she thought of her. Holding the baby a little closer as if to protect her from the nastiness, she watched Ethan and saw a flash of anger in his eyes. It was a wonder Alice didn't bother to notice it, as well.

"I'm a housekeeper, not a babysitter," Alice said again.

"I heard you the first time," Ethan said, and Sadie heard the warning in his tone.

"As long as you remember it," the woman snapped. "Now, I'll be having my dinner in my kitchen. As I didn't know you'd be home, or bringing along company—" her gaze swept over Sadie and the baby dismissively "—I didn't prepare a meal for you. I'm not a babysitter and I'm not a cook."

"Here's something else you're not," Ethan interrupted. "Employed."

"I beg your pardon?" Alice bleated.

"You should," Ethan retorted, "but I doubt you really are. You're fired. Get your stuff and get out."

"What?" Sadie said.

She couldn't believe this. For years, she'd thought he should get rid of Alice. But to do it today? When everything was already in turmoil? What had happened to "change is bad"?

Alice's whole body stiffened as if someone had shoved a pole down the back of her grim black dress. Clearly indignant, she lifted her chin and glared at Ethan. "I see no reason for this—"

Ethan took a step closer to her and the woman backed up. Alice was in no physical danger and she had to know that, but seeing Ethan's temper was so rare, it was startling when it finally appeared.

"This is my house, Alice. Not yours," he said. "Something you seem to have forgotten over the years."

"I don't know what you mean…"

"Yes, you do." Ethan loomed over her, using his height as an intimidation factor. "Do you really think I haven't noticed that you've crowned yourself queen of *my* house?"

The woman's eyes darted from side to side as if looking for an escape—but she didn't find one.

"I've been willing to put up with your attitude because, frankly, you didn't matter enough to make a change. But that ends now," Ethan told her. "This is *my* house. And I'll run it however the hell I want to run it. And I'll hire someone who's more concerned with her job than she is with pretending she's the lady of the manor."

Alice sputtered and Sadie ducked her head to hide a smile. She really shouldn't be pleased about this, but Alice had had this coming for a long time. Plus, Ethan was the sexiest show she'd ever seen. Anger rippled off him in hot waves, yet he spoke so quietly, so coolly. It was the contrast, really, that was making Sadie feel as if her nerve endings were electrified.

Well, that and the look in his eyes. The man was so hot that smoke should have been lifting off the top of his head. He was definitely her weakness.

"You owe me two weeks' salary," Alice snapped.

"You're right." Ethan started for the stairs, already putting the awful woman in the past. "Leave an address on the entry table and I'll mail you a check and a severance bonus."

"A bonus?" Sadie said quietly, as she followed after him.

"It's worth it," Ethan muttered.

"See?" Sadie countered, her voice as quiet as his. "Like I told you. Not all change is bad."

He shot her a look. "Save it."

By the time they got the baby settled in her room, Ethan was even more on edge. He'd fired his housekeeper, been saddled with a baby and his assistant had resigned.

"Hell of a day," he muttered.

"A long one, anyway," Sadie agreed. "At least the baby's room looks beautiful. Well, except for that beige paint. That should be changed to something a little more girlie."

"I'm not having a pink room in my house," he argued, walking down the stairs behind her. His gaze dropped to the curve of her butt and his hands itched to grab hold and squeeze. Actually, what he really wanted to do was get her out of her work clothes, stretch her out on the floor in front of the fire and explore every square inch of that tidy body.

"I didn't say pink," she said, tossing him a look

over her shoulder. "That's a little sexist, don't you think?"

"I didn't know a color *could* be sexist."

"Well," she quipped, "now you do. I was thinking something cheerful, bright. Pale yellow, maybe, or a soft green. With pictures and maybe a mural. Something to stimulate her."

He snorted a laugh. "The way she screamed when you put her in the crib tells me she's already plenty stimulated."

At the bottom of the stairs, Sadie stopped and turned around to look at him. "She's lost her parents, been thrown at people she doesn't know and forced to sleep in a bed she doesn't recognize. I'd like to see how well either of us would handle that situation."

There were actual sparks in her eyes as she glared at him. Ethan held up both hands. "You're right."

Astonishment flashed across her features. "Wow. I'm right. A banner day indeed."

"There's that sarcasm again. What does it say that I'm starting to enjoy it?"

"That you're a glutton for punishment?" She grinned, turned around and marched across the foyer to the front table, which held a massive crystal vase and a fall flower arrangement. She picked up her brown leather bag and slung it over her shoulder.

Suspicion washed over him as he demanded, "What are you doing?"

"I'm going home."

A feeling he didn't want to describe as "panic" washed over him. He glanced down at the baby monitor in his hand as if it were a live grenade. "You can't leave."

"Sure I can." She gave him a smile that punched at his insides. "Don't worry, thanks to that bonus, I'm staying for an extra month, remember? I'll see you tomorrow."

He threw a quick look at the stairs behind him. There was a baby on the second floor and if Sadie left, *he* was the only one here to take care of it. *Her.*

Unacceptable.

How had this happened to him? He, who so carefully regimented the world around him. This morning, his life had been just as he wanted it. A successful business, an efficient assistant, no bumps or twists on a road that lay before him, straight and narrow. And now…everything was a tangled mess and damned if he'd suffer through this alone. "Stay."

"I am."

"No," he said tightly, knowing she was referring to staying on at the office, and helping him find a damn nanny. He meant so much more. "Stay here. At the house."

A flash of something interesting darted across her eyes and was gone again in a blink. "You want me to stay the night?"

"No," he corrected, making sure she understood. "I want you to stay here at the house with me. Help me with that baby until I find a damn nanny or hire a housekeeper who isn't allergic to children."

She laughed a little and shook her head hard enough to send those loose blond curls into a dance around her head. "Not a chance."

Her laughter was both erotic and extremely annoying. Sadie was about to walk out that door, leaving him alone in the house with a child. Cowardly or not, Ethan had no problem acknowledging that he did *not* want to be alone with that baby.

Earlier that day, he'd given Sadie a lot of money to get her to stay an extra month. Maybe all he really needed to do here was offer even more. Hell, money was easy for him—asking for help wasn't.

"I'll pay you fifty thousand dollars extra to move in here temporarily."

"What?" She stared at him.

"You heard me." At least he had her attention. She hadn't left yet, and that was good.

"I did. I just don't believe it."

"Well, believe it." Ethan pushed one hand through his hair briefly. "Look, I don't like admitting this, but when it comes to that baby I'm out of my depth. I need your help."

Her head snapped back and a small smile curved her mouth. At any other time, he would have enjoyed that soft smile.

"You're saying that there's something Ethan Hart can't handle."

He scowled at her. "You're enjoying this, aren't you?"

"A little."

This was new territory for Ethan. He was self-sufficient. In charge. Yet now, an infant had reduced him to admitting his failings. "Fine. Yes. I need your help. So what do you say?"

She tipped her head to one side and her short blond curls fell lazily with the movement. "For fifty thousand dollars, of course I'll stay."

Pleased, but a little surprised that she'd given in so easily, he wondered why money was such a motivator for her. Was there something going on in her life that he didn't know about? "I didn't expect you to agree so quickly. Who knew you were so mercenary?"

She laughed shortly. "Mercenary? That may be how it looks to you, but I've got news for you. Maybe it's not the same for gazillionaires, but the rest of us peons have to make mortgage payments, car payments, buy, you know, *food*. This money will let me take my time finding a new job. Help me get a new car, maybe fix the plumbing in my condo…"

He didn't much care for the "finding a new job" thing, but for the rest, he realized he hadn't taken any interest in Sadie's life before now. He should have. The car she had strapped the baby into was a nearly fifteen-year-old sedan. Why was she driving such an old car? And her condo had plumbing issues? Hell, until today he didn't know she *owned* a condo.

They'd worked together closely for five years and she was a mystery to him. His own fault, he told himself. He'd been so attracted to her that he'd treated her as if she were invisible. He hadn't taken an interest in her because he couldn't *afford* to. Since she'd turned in her resignation a few hours ago, it was as if he were meeting her for the first time.

The desire was there and stronger than ever— but there was also something new. Damned if he didn't *like* her.

Well he felt like an ass. It didn't happen often, thank God, but Ethan could admit to it when it did. At least to himself. Offering her money had been a last-ditch effort for him to keep her in her job. To keep her here, where she could help him out with that baby. He hadn't even realized how important that money could be to her. He paid his employees well and never really thought about it otherwise. He'd grown up wealthy and intended to stay that way. So when you were used to a lot of money being readily available, you didn't often stop to think that money might be an issue for someone else.

She was still watching him. Waiting. Finally, he said, "Fine. I admit it. You're the hero of the working class and I'm a cold money grubber."

"That sounds about right." She grinned and that smile punched him in the solar plexus so hard he had to fight for air. "I mean, come on. You're paying me a hundred and fifty thousand dollars to help you out for a month. Normal people don't do that."

"Now I'm not normal?"

She laughed again and it irritated him just how much he enjoyed the sound.

"Of course you're not."

"Thanks very much," he muttered darkly.

"I didn't say you were *abnormal*," she said. Digging into her purse, she pulled her keys out and jangled them in her palm. "For example. Most people don't live in mansions."

"I know that."

"Do you?" She tipped her head to one side again and Ethan realized just how often she did that when talking to him. And he also realized how fascinated he was with those loose blond curls and how they moved. He wondered how they would feel sliding across his skin.

"You realize the bonus you offered me today is more than most people make in a year."

He frowned and shook himself out of the distraction of her hair. Focusing, he said, "I'm not completely clueless, Sadie." Then he noticed the car keys in her hand. "Where are you going? You just agreed to stay *here*."

"Not without clothes."

Okay, that short sentence opened up a world of images in his mind. Sadie, walking through his house naked. Sadie in the shower, water sliding down her skin. Sadie stretched out across his bed, holding her arms up to him. Sadie beneath him, crying out his name as he slammed his body into hers.

Ethan swallowed hard, took a breath and blew it out again. Man, once he'd unleashed all the sexual thoughts about her he'd been suppressing for years, they were almost too much to take. He came back to the present in time to see her headed for the door. She paused and looked back over her shoulder. "I'm going home to pack a bag. I'll be back."

He couldn't stop himself from shooting a worried glance at the staircase that led to the ticking time bomb upstairs. Shifting his gaze back to Sadie's, he said, "An extra twenty-five thousand if you make it back before she wakes up and starts screaming again."

"Stop throwing money at me." She laughed and the sound bubbled through his bloodstream like champagne. "You're really off your game, aren't you?"

"Will it get you back here fast if I say yes?"

"Relax. I'll be back in an hour or so." She opened the door, stepped onto the porch, then added, "Emma's not going to kill you, Ethan."

When she left, closing the door behind her, Ethan muttered, "Don't bet on it."

"I'm still not sure about this."

Gabriel stood outside the Heart Chocolates offices

and looked up at the building as if he'd never seen it before. He'd done a lot of thinking about this plan and he was still torn about what to do.

Not surprising, really. He was a Hart, after all, even if he was the younger brother. He'd grown up with the same family stories Ethan had heard. He'd been taught to respect what had come before and build on the traditions already set in stone.

But wasn't that what he was trying to do? Build on what had been left to them? If they went Ethan's route, they would continue to be successful—at least in the short term. But if they didn't grow and build on what had been left in their care, would they be doing justice to the great-grandfather who had started it all?

Behind him, on Pacific Coast Highway, traffic whizzed past in a never-ending stream. He turned to watch the life pulsing on the street and the cold, January wind slapped his face. Winter nights came early, but that didn't mean people avoided coming to the beach. Out on the sand tonight there would be flames dancing in fire pits, barbecues and music pumping into the night.

When he was a kid, he'd been a member of the never-ending party at the beach. But right here, right now, all Gabe could think about was what he was about to do.

For generations, his family had guarded their chocolate recipe like the Holy Grail. Was he really willing to be the first Hart to share that recipe with an outsider?

"Gabe…" Pam took his hand and gave it a squeeze, as if she could sense his uncertainty. "You're not betraying anyone. You're trying to help. To make a difference."

"Yeah," he mused wryly, "not sure Ethan would see it like that."

"This isn't about Ethan," she said softly. "But honestly, if you don't feel right about this, then don't do it."

He looked down into her brown eyes. The streetlights threw shadows across her face and made her eyes seem even deeper, darker, than they usually were. Gabe held on to her hand like a lifeline. "No, I have to. But trust me, once Ethan finds out what I did. This could tear us so far apart we might never find our way back to each other. And yeah, I know he's a pain in the ass, but he's my brother."

A cold, damp wind rushed past them, lifting Pam's hair into twisting black strands. A rush of heat and something more filled Gabe, and he held on to it, to distract him from what he was about to do. He read the sympathy on her face and held on to that, as well.

He tried to make her understand how he was feeling about all of this. As much as Gabe wanted to try out his ideas, to push his brother into stepping into the twenty-first century, it went against everything he was to sneak into the office and take that recipe. His whole life, he'd been raised with the notion that family was more important than anything. That their family legacy was to be honored. Defended. But essentially, wasn't that what he was trying to do?

Rubbing one hand across his eyes, Gabriel murmured, "You know, Ethan's been the head of the family since our dad died. He's taken care of everything. Put me through college and worked here, running everything by himself until I was ready to come on board."

"And the minute you did, his thumb came down on top of you," she reminded him. "I can't remember how many times you've told me about Ethan squashing your ideas."

Gabe winced. It did feel like that sometimes, but he knew what Ethan dealt with. It wasn't just about maintaining the Hart family legacy… It was dealing with buyers, merchants, marketing, and God knew what else, just to keep moving forward. If Gabe went through with this tonight, what else could it be but a betrayal?

"Maybe I made it sound worse than it is," he mused.

"I know all about family, Gabe. And yes, my brother drives me nuts, too. But really, this comes down to you. You're having second thoughts," Pam said, holding his hand between both of hers.

"And third and fourth," he said, agreeing with her

as he took an even longer look at the building that held his family's heritage.

It was brick, which made it stand out in the middle of Newport Beach. Probably not a good idea to build with brick in earthquake country, Gabe silently admitted. But his grandfather had insisted the brick looked sturdy. Dependable. As he wanted their then-fledgling company to be. And Gabe had to admit he must have been onto something because but for a few falling bricks and a couple cracked windows in the last big quake, the building was still standing. Just like the Hart family itself.

But would the family connection survive Gabe going behind Ethan's back to prove a point? And if he didn't go through with this, see his own ideas through, would Gabe eventually resent Ethan enough to destroy their relationship completely?

Questions he wished he had answers to.

"Gabe?" Pam's voice cut into his thoughts and he could have kissed her for it.

"Yeah?"

"You're not doing this *to* Ethan. You're doing it *for* Ethan."

His mouth quirked briefly. He knew damn well his big brother wouldn't see it like that.

She wasn't finished, though. "Like I said before, I understand family loyalty, Gabe. I really do. But sometimes, you have to do what you know is right, whether the family agrees or not. This is your chance to prove something—not just to Ethan, but to your-self."

Pam was right and Gabe knew it, though he wasn't thrilled about it. Still, if he didn't try making up those new flavors, following through on his idea, he'd always regret it. He had to know that he'd done what he could to make his own vision a reality. After all, if *he* didn't have faith in his vision, how could he hope to convince Ethan?

Pam reached up and cupped his cheek in the palm of her hand. "But if you don't want to do this…"

"I really don't," he said, bending down to give her a quick, hard kiss that scrambled his brain cells even as it steadied him. "But I also don't have a choice."

"Are you sure, Gabe?" she asked, biting her bottom lip in a sure sign that she was anxious. "I'll back you either way. You could even wait for a better time. I didn't mean to rush you into this by suggesting we take the recipe to a chocolate chef I know."

"You didn't push me into this," he assured her. "Don't think that. The idea to make up some of the new flavors was a good one. But I'm doing this for me, Pam. If I don't try, I'll never know."

She studied him for a long minute, then nodded. "Okay, then. I'm with you."

"Yeah," he said, smiling. "You really are."

He slung one arm around her shoulders and hugged her tight before steering her toward the glass doors. Gabe already knew Ethan wasn't at the office.

His car wasn't in the parking lot, so the coast, as they said in old movies, was clear.

The security guard in the foyer leaped to his feet to unlock the door as Gabriel approached. Once they were inside, the door was closed and locked again. Light streamed down on the gleaming, honey-toned wood floor. The walls were splashed with colorful pictures of their chocolates.

"Evening, Mr. Hart," the guard said. "Didn't expect to see you back here tonight."

"I won't be long, Joe," he said, and guided Pam to the elevator. "Just have to go get something from the office."

"Yes, sir." The older man went back to his desk and wasn't even looking at them when the elevator doors hissed closed.

The office was too quiet. It felt as if they were walking through an upscale abandoned building. Their shoes on the hardwood floors clacked noisily in the stillness. The lights were dimmed and in every shadow, Gabe imagined he could see his great-grandfather and all the other Harts who'd come before him watching with disapproval. But he shook that off and continued into Ethan's office.

The original recipe had, of course, been scanned into the computer and was kept in an encrypted file that only Ethan and Gabriel could access. It was also stored on flash drives kept in several different places, for security's sake. And because he was

Ethan, Gabriel's big brother kept the original recipe in a bank box, and a copy of it in a wall safe. He did it because their father had done it that way, too. As if keeping that recipe close would continue the company's growth.

Though it wasn't a plea to the universe for luck. It was more of a family talisman.

And Gabriel was about to set it free.

Four

Sadie was running late, but she stopped at her brother's house, anyway. She told herself it was sort of on the way to Dana Point from her condo in Long Beach, so it wasn't as if she'd gone very far out of her way. Fine, it was *way* out of the way. But the truth was, she just wanted to talk to Gina.

Mike and Gina's house was in a subdivision in Foothill Ranch. The houses were big, but rooms were small. The neighborhoods were laid out in curving, twisting streets and the houses sat practically on the curb. No room for a front yard or a driveway. The backyards were small, too, but the streets were crowded with herds of children. Which was really why her brother and his wife were still in the house they were outgrowing.

Still, every time she turned onto their street, with the cookie-cutter houses lined up like pale beige soldiers, Sadie thought of the opening shots of the old movie *Poltergeist*.

"Hey! Nice surprise!" Gina opened the front door, reached out to hug her, then dragged Sadie into the house. "How did you escape your captor?"

Sadie laughed. Mike and Gina were not big fans of Ethan. "There've been a lot of surprises today. That's why I'm here. Had to talk to you about it."

"Oh, now I'm intrigued." Gina grinned and tucked her shoulder-length black hair behind her ears. She wore faded jeans, one of Mike's long-sleeved white shirts that, on Gina, hung down past her thighs, and she was barefoot. Her daughter was only three weeks old and already Gina looked fabulous. "Come on in, sit by the fire and spill your guts."

"Lovely invitation." Sadie glanced at the stairs. "The kids in bed already?"

"Don't jinx me," Gina warned, holding up one finger to her lips. "I wore the boys out at the park today and the baby's in one of her four-hour sleep jags. So let's take advantage of it. You want some wine?"

"So much." Sadie dropped her purse on the dining room table and followed Gina into the kitchen. Through the wall of windows behind the sink, Sadie looked out at the greenbelt and the yellow lab, Einstein, who was sprawled across the grass, taking a nap.

The house, this place, was cozy. There were toys on the patio, a trampoline in one corner of the yard and tiny sneakers kicked off beside the back door. It was family. It was exactly what Sadie wanted for herself. And finally, she'd set herself on the path toward getting it.

"What's going on?" Gina handed her a glass of wine, took one for herself, then led the way to the couch lined up in front of a gas fireplace that was hissing merrily.

Sadie told her. All of it. As she talked, she watched Gina's reactions and was glad to see that most of them matched what she'd been feeling herself.

"I don't know what to comment on first," Gina finally said, when Sadie ran down.

"Dealer's choice." Sadie took a long sip, then got up to grab a bag of chips from the pantry.

"Okay, *wow* on the money front. I mean, whether he knows it or not, Ethan just helped you quit."

"I know." Sadie plopped down beside her friend. "I don't think he realizes that yet."

"Eventually he will and he won't be happy." Gina reached out and patted Sadie's hand. "But honey, this is great. You'll be able to take some time before you jump back into another job. And get a new car before the one you have breaks down around you and you're left sitting on the street clutching a steering wheel."

Sad, but true. "That's what I was thinking."

"Plus you won't be held hostage at a chocolate factory anymore, so maybe we could set you up with Mike's friend Josh." Gina grinned and winked at her. "He's really great. Gorgeous. Beautiful eyes, fantastic butt."

"Aren't you married to my brother?"

"Please. Was I struck blind lately?" Gina rolled her eyes. "Anyway, Josh joined the fire department a month ago and Mike really likes him."

Mike was a firefighter, which meant he was gone for four days, then home for four days. Since they all spent so much time together, Mike got to know the guys at his station really well. But this was the first time he and Gina had tried to set Sadie up with one of them.

"Wow. A setup. That's a first."

"Well, come on, what would have been the point before?" Gina shook her head slowly. "You were always working. Why bother setting you up? Heck, you walked out of Megan's wedding for your job."

Sadie winced. "I just reminded Ethan of that today."

Gina curled her legs up under her and leaned back on the couch. "Sweetie, this is your chance to have a life. What're you looking so worried about?"

"Do I?"

"Your forehead's all wrinkled up. You should stop that."

Instinctively Sadie reached up and smoothed her fingers across her brow. "I'm not worried. I'm…" She sighed. "I don't know what I am. It's been a weird day."

"You could say that," Gina said with a laugh. "Resigned, helping take care of a baby, poor little thing, and lots of cash."

"And," Sadie mused, "once I quit, Ethan looked at me differently."

Gina snorted. "You mean he noticed you were female?"

"Exactly." Sophie took another sip of the cold white wine. "It was…exciting."

Gina slapped one hand to her forehead. "Oh, God."

"What?"

"Sadie, the whole point of quitting was so you could find a life, right?" Gina reached out, grabbed her hand and shook it. "Didn't you tell me two weeks ago that you want to find the right guy for you and give up on the fantasy of Ethan?"

God, it was humiliating to have her own words tossed back at her. But this was why she'd come to Gina. To get the truth. Hard as it was to hear. Mike and Gina had the kind of relationship that Sadie wanted for herself. They were partners. They laughed. They fought. They loved and always had each other's back. And Sadie wasn't blind. She'd seen the looks her brother gave his wife when he thought no one was watching.

She wanted to be wanted like that.

"Yeah, I did." Sadie looked down into her wine. "But…"

"Do you still have your list?" Gina asked.

"Of course." Sadie had been working on that list for the last two years.

"How many qualifications are on it now?"

"Five," Sadie said, staring down into her glass. When she first made up the list of what she wanted in a man, there'd been more than twenty items on it. Over time, though, she'd whittled it down to the top five.

"Let's hear them."

Sadie knew what her sister-in-law was up to. She wanted to remind Sadie that Ethan was *not* the man for her. And maybe Gina was right. Today had been fun. Watching Ethan's panic, sharing things outside the job with him. Seeing him fire Alice and take charge of a child he hadn't wanted. It was as if they'd been a team of a different sort today. Not the work thing, where they each knew their roles and acted them out effortlessly.

This had been different. Today they'd been simply Ethan and Sadie. Man and woman. And she'd enjoyed it way too much. So it would probably be a good thing if she reminded *herself* about her list.

"Fine." She ticked them off on her fingers. "Sexy. Adventurous. Sense of humor. Spending time with me. Loves kids."

"Uh-huh," Gina mused. "And how many of those fit Ethan?"

"Sexy…" Her voice trailed off, because she couldn't say more. "Okay, fine. He's not the man on my list."

"Thank you." Nodding at her, Gina said with some sympathy, "Sadie, I know you're nuts about the man, but you deserve someone to be nuts about *you*."

"Yeah. I know. But—"

"No buts," Gina interrupted, holding up one hand to keep her quiet. "Ethan's not going to give you what you want."

"What if all I want is hot sex?"

Gina laughed and set her glass down. "Who doesn't want that? But it's not *all* you want."

"No, it's not." But oh boy, it was a great idea. Just imagining hot, wild sex with Ethan set off tiny fires inside her. She took a drink of the cold wine, hoping to smooth things out. It didn't work.

"Still, not a bad idea." Gina shrugged and took another sip of her own wine. "If you think it'll help, get the hot sex from Ethan, then when you finally leave your job, you walk with no regrets. No what-if's running through your head. Sadie, it's long past time to look out for yourself."

More heat rushed through Sadie at the thought of hot sex with Ethan. But then, she'd been feeling that rush for five years. Was Gina right? Should she take advantage of her "resigned but still with him" situation? She *really* wanted to. Even if her future wouldn't include the man she'd loved for so long… the present could be pretty great.

"Good," Gina said. "You're thinking about it. And from what I can see, you like the idea. But don't think too long," she warned. "Sometimes you think yourself right out of doing what you want to do."

Sadie fell back against the couch. "It's really annoying that you know me so well."

"That's so sweet."

Sadie laughed just as a baby's wail drifted through the monitor sitting on the coffee table. Gina sighed. "Playtime's over. You sure you don't want to stay here tonight and go rescue Ethan in the morning? Mike's shift won't be over for two more days and I could use the company."

"Tempting," Sadie said, "but Ethan offered me another twenty-five thousand if I made it back before Emma woke up."

Gina's laugh rolled out loud and hard. "The man's really desperate, isn't he? Okay, fine. But once you're really out of a job, your nephews would love to spend some time with you."

"Disneyland trip on me," Sadie promised, then leaned in to give Gina a hug. "Then I'll camp out here with you when Mike's on shift."

"Good, that sounds great."

"Thanks," Sadie said. "Seriously."

"I didn't do much."

"You married my dumb brother just because you knew I needed a sister," Sadie teased.

"Yeah, that's why I did it. And the hot sex, of course."

"Well, naturally."

If she hadn't been so damn efficient, Sadie could have been on the road toward Ethan's house. Instead, she was stopping by the office to pick up the file on the Donatello acquisition. Since the meeting had been postponed until tomorrow, she and Ethan could go over the basics again tonight.

Joe let her in the front door and she headed straight for the elevators. Time was ticking. She'd stayed too long with Gina, but it had felt good to have her sister-in-law back her up. Of course, no surprise there. Gina had been after Sadie to quit her job for the last two years so she could have a life outside the office.

And Gina was right. Sadie knew it, even though she didn't like it. Stepping off the elevator, Sadie looked around the place that had pretty much been her world for the last five years. It wasn't the first time she'd been in the building long after everyone else had left for the day. She couldn't count how many times she and Ethan had worked late, just the two of them in the quiet.

This time, it felt different to her. Not only because she was here alone, but because now she knew she wouldn't be here much longer. In another month or so, she'd be gone from her job, this office, Ethan's life. She felt a small pang of regret at that thought, but leaving was really her only choice if she wanted more for herself than a good-paying job.

She started walking toward Ethan's office. The lights were dim, cubicles quiet and the air still smelled of the day's coffee. It was empty, of course, but for the memories that crowded around her. "It's going to be weird to not come here every day," she whispered, and shivered a little as her voice dissolved in the silence.

Sadie shook off the thought and her own mixed feelings as she opened Ethan's office door and said, "Gabe? What're you doing here?"

Startled, Gabriel jumped, then laughed shortly. "God, you scared the hell out of me."

The woman with him was pretty, with long black hair and big brown eyes. As Sadie watched, she moved in closer to Gabe, standing beside the bank of wide windows. "Hi," she said. "I'm Pam. Pam Cassini."

"Right, sorry." Gabe shook his head and dropped one arm around Pam's shoulders. "Seriously, Sadie, you move so quietly I didn't hear you coming in. What're you doing here?"

"I wanted to pick up a file to take to Ethan's."

He looked confused. "You're going to Ethan's house?"

"Yeah," she said, walking across the room to the

wall of wooden cabinets. Opening the top one, she flipped through the files inside until she found Donatello's and pulled it out before shutting the cabinet again. Sure, they had all the files on computers and backed up by the cloud, and any number of other security measures. But they still kept hard copies, too. So much easier to read through.

"It's a long story," she said, "so I'll let Ethan tell you about it. But bottom line, he's been named guardian of a six-month-old girl."

"Ethan?" Gabriel's shock was understandable. Ethan wasn't exactly father-of-the-year material. "My brother's taking care of an infant?"

Sadie laughed a little. "With my help. But why are you guys here?"

Gabe looked at Pam briefly, then shrugged and said, "I wanted to show Pam around and Ethan's office has the best view."

It did. But not at night. Odd, but it wasn't her business why one of the owners might be in the office after closing. After all, *she* was there, right?

"Okay. Well," she said, waving the file, "I'd better get moving. I'll see you tomorrow, Gabe. Nice meeting you," she added to Pam, who smiled and nodded.

She was in the lobby, still wondering what was going on with Gabriel, when her cell phone rang. "Thanks, Joe," she said, slipping out the door before glancing at the phone screen.

Grinning to herself, she answered. "Hello, Ethan."

"Are you on your way back?" he demanded. "She's making noises. I think she's waking up."

"On my way." This situation was really far more entertaining than it should be. But Sadie couldn't help enjoying seeing the man who was always calm, cool and in charge suddenly thrown off balance by a baby. She unlocked her car, slid in and fired it up. "Be there in twenty minutes, and don't offer me more money if I can get there in fifteen."

"Just get here."

Still smiling to herself, Sadie shook her head and steered into the never-ending traffic on Pacific Coast Highway.

"She's asleep again," Sadie told him a half hour later. "I just patted her back for a while and she drifted off."

"Good." Ethan grabbed a beer out of the fridge. "Do you want anything?"

Oh, so many things, Sadie thought. Starting with, of course, that hot sex she'd been talking about with Gina. Looking at him now, she found it astonishing to realize just how sexy the man looked in a pair of jeans and an untucked blue dress shirt. She'd only ever seen him in one of the elegant suits Sadie had sort of assumed he had been born in.

God knew he was sexy as sin in one of his suits, but seeing him here, dressed so casually, put a whole new spin on her fantasies. Her mouth watered and her heartbeat kicked up a notch. Then she took a breath, pushed her fantasy aside and said, "Food, Ethan. I want food."

He nodded. "I had Chinese delivered. It's in the oven."

"Perfect." Sadie got it and set everything out on the table, then opened a half-dozen cabinets before she found plates.

Ethan found silverware, opened a bottle of wine and got each of them water besides. In a few minutes, they were sitting opposite each other in the soft, overhead light. The kitchen, like the rest of the house, was huge.

It was white—boring—with gray cabinets and a mile and a half of black granite counters. They were so tidy it looked as though no one used the room at all, and that was probably true. Alice had said herself she wasn't a cook, and Sadie was willing to bet that though he could order takeout, Ethan wouldn't have the first clue how to cook for himself.

The table sat in front of windows that overlooked the backyard and the ocean beyond. At night, though, like now, there were solar-powered lights shining beneath bushes, under trees and along a path that led down the slope toward the cliff's edge.

As she thought of that, Sadie said, "You're going to have to put a fence in at the end of the yard. Once Emma starts getting around, it won't be safe the way it is."

"Already thought of that," he said, helping himself to a serving of cashew chicken. "While you were gone, I called the contractor who did the remodel here a couple of years ago. He's coming out tomorrow to do the measurements."

Impressed, Sadie said, "That was quick."

Wryly, Ethan responded, "I may not know how to diaper a child, but I do know how to keep it safe."

"Her."

"Her." He took a bite, glared at Sadie and said, "What took you so long?"

She dived into her beef and broccoli—that was a point for Ethan. He remembered her favorite from all those times they'd had dinner in his office while they worked. "After I got my stuff, I stopped at my brother's house to talk to Gina."

"To tell her you resigned?"

"Yes," she said, "and other things." She wasn't about to admit to him that Gina had suggested using him for hot monkey sex. Although now that the thought had settled into her mind again, the suggestion was sounding better and better.

"And was Gina happy to hear it?"

Sadie looked up and met his eyes. The overhead lamp shone down on his face, creating shadows, but strangely, it also illuminated. Everything inside her turned upside down. It had always been that way with Ethan. One look from him and she was quivering inside. It was humiliating to admit, even to herself, since he seemed completely unaware of her as a person—let alone a *woman*.

"Yeah," she finally said, taking a sip of wine before digging into the fried rice. "She was glad I quit."

"Nice that your family's happy about you being unemployed."

Her eyebrows lifted. "That's because she knows I won't be for long. What they're happy about is that maybe now they'll get to see me occasionally."

He dropped his fork and it clattered onto the fine china plate. "You make it sound as if you were an indentured servant. It wasn't that bad."

"Megan's wedding," she said.

"One time," he countered.

"Hardly. I couldn't get to the hospital for any of Mike and Gina's kids' births, either," she reminded him.

"And this is all my fault." His tone clearly said he didn't think so.

"Partly," Sadie said, reaching for her glass of water. She took a long drink, then said, "Mostly mine, though." Meeting his gaze across the table, she continued. "I could have said no to you. I could have told you that I wouldn't work all hours. Or that I wouldn't leave Megan's wedding."

He studied her and she wished she could tell what he was thinking. But he'd sat back in his chair and now his eyes were shadowed, too, hiding what he was feeling.

"I didn't, though, because I liked my job, Ethan." Well, that was true as far as it went. But it wasn't what had caused her to come running whenever Ethan called. That was something else.

Wanting to be with him, around him, working and talking with him.

She didn't mind the late nights because she and Ethan were together, solving problems, making plans for the company's future. She'd fooled herself into believing there was more between them than there was. Her own imagination and desires had convinced her that one day he would notice her.

Well, that had never happened.

"And," she went on, "since I liked it, I sort of let it take over my life."

"Thanks for that, anyway," he muttered.

"Wasn't finished," she added, waving her fork at him. "You do the same thing, Ethan. You don't have a life outside the business."

"So you said earlier." He pushed the plate in front of him to one side. "But my life is just how I like it."

She looked around the kitchen, which was so tidy it could have been in an empty model home. "Really? You like being one man living in a house big enough for ten or twenty people?"

"I like the quiet."

"Right." She laughed shortly and pushed her own plate aside. Here in the darkness, it felt intimate, sitting so close to him. With no one to interrupt, she felt as though she could actually say a few things that she'd wanted to over the years. "You're hiding, Ethan."

"Hiding? From whom?" A bark of laughter shot from his throat. "That's ridiculous."

She shook her head slowly. "No, it's not. Ever since your divorce, you shut yourself off from everything."

Even in the dim light she could see his features freeze up. His laughter abruptly ended, and his mouth flattened into a grim line. "We're not talking about that."

"Of course not. You never have." Forearms braced on the table, she leaned toward him. "This time, though, you don't have to. I will," she said with a shrug.

"You're full of yourself after turning in that resignation," he said.

She nodded. "That's fair. Like I said, it's very freeing."

He didn't smile. "Think you can say anything you want, and I suppose you can. But I don't have to listen."

Her head tipped to one side. "Hiding again?"

"Not hiding," he said shortly. "Just not interested in *sharing*."

She sat back. Picking up her wine, Sadie took a sip, then asked, "What are you interested in, Ethan?"

"My company."

"And?"

"And what? That's it," he said, and stood up. He carried his plate to the sink, turned around and looked at her. "My family started this business more than a hundred years ago and it's up to me to keep it at the top. To protect it. And since when do the two of us talk about this stuff?"

"Since I quit and I don't have to worry about my boss firing me." Sadie carried her plate to the sink, too, and stood beside him.

"I can still tell you to get out."

"But you won't." She pointed to the baby monitor standing in the center of the black granite island.

He gritted his teeth so hard the muscle in his jaw twitched. "Think you're safe, do you?"

"Actually, yes, I do." Turning around, she leaned back against the counter, bracing her hands on the cold, hard edge. She tilted her head to one side and noticed a brief flash of something in his eyes.

"You realize you're still working for me for the next month…"

"Sure," she said, "but that's unofficial."

"I'm paying a lot of money for 'unofficial'."

"I'm worth it," she quipped, and saw that flash in his eyes again. However briefly it had appeared, it set off a similar flash inside her. Sadie felt heat puddle in the pit of her stomach and then slide slowly south. A deep throbbing began at her core as she stared up into his eyes, and it took every bit of her self-control to keep from moving to try to ease that ache.

"I suppose you are." His words came in a whisper and his eyes looked suddenly deep, dark and filled with emotions she couldn't read.

Sadie would have given a lot to know what he was thinking, but in the next moment, she got her first clue.

"It's strange," he said.

"There's been a lot of strange today," she said softly. "Can you be more specific?"

"Okay. I think this is the first time I've ever seen you out of your work clothes…"

Sadie glanced down. She wore black jeans, a long-sleeved red T-shirt and black ballet flats. Hardly an outfit worth putting that look of interest on his face, but there it was.

"And you're barefoot, wearing jeans. I didn't know you *owned* jeans," she said. God, he was barefoot. That was sexy, too. *Get a grip, Sadie.* "It's the first time we've been together when we're *not* working."

"Not true." He put his hands on either side of her and loomed in close. "There was that trip to Dublin last summer."

"A business trip," she murmured, and felt his heat drifting toward her. He was doing this on purpose. Why was he doing this? And oh, she hoped he didn't stop.

"What about when we had a drink in that pub after the meeting?"

"Still work," she said, and she had to look up to meet his gaze as he loomed over her. Her brain instantly painted another picture where he would be looking down at her. Where his body would cover hers. Where his mouth would be on hers as they came together in the most intimate way possible.

"And the singing?" he asked, and she dragged her focus back to the conversation at hand.

"Work but fun," she said, remembering that night in Ireland as one of the best out of the last five years.

"So you can at least admit you had fun that night."

"Never said I didn't."

"Uh-huh. Are you having fun *now*?" he asked, bending his head a little closer to hers.

"I could be, if I knew what you were up to," Sadie admitted, staring into his eyes and trying to decipher what was behind all this. "But I think *you* are having fun."

"Oh, I am," he assured her, as his gaze moved over her features.

"Why are you doing this?" she asked, and could have kicked herself. Did it really matter *why*? Having his mouth just a breath from hers, having his gaze locked on her, was something she'd thought about for years, and now that it was happening she questioned it? What was *wrong* with her?

"Am I making you nervous?" Ethan asked in response.

"If you were?"

"Then I'd stop."

"Then I'm not nervous."

"Glad to hear it." Suddenly any trace of humor was gone from his eyes. His features were taut as he stared at her as if seeing her for the first time. When he leaned in closer, so did Sadie.

Her breath was gone. And she didn't care. She could hear her own heart pounding, felt it hammering in her chest, but breathing was simply off the table. Her blood rushed through her veins, then headed south to set up camp in her groin. Heated throbbing took over, along with an ache she knew all too well. She wanted him, and now it looked like she might have him, and her body was reacting with bursts of internal joy.

"I've thought about doing this," he whispered.

"Me, too," Sadie said softly.

"Yeah?" One corner of his mouth lifted. "I didn't because you worked for me. But now you don't."

"Good point," she agreed. She stared into his eyes, lowered her gaze to his mouth and then back up again. "So, are you going to kiss me or what?"

"Stop talking, Sadie." Then he kissed her.

Five

That first touch of his lips to hers was electric. Sadie's whole body lit up like a neon festival. He cupped her face with his hands, tilted her head and took more. He parted her lips with his tongue and she met that intimate caress with eagerness. It was everything she'd thought it would be and more.

Pulling her close, Ethan held her pressed against his chest as his hands moved to stroke her, touch her. Everywhere. He grabbed hold of her behind and squeezed, sending new tendrils of excitement scattering through her cells.

She moved in even closer to him, twined her arms around his neck and held on while their mouths met and danced and promised each other more.

Hot sex with Ethan.

That one thought blazed across her mind and she groaned as Ethan tore his mouth from hers to drag his lips and tongue along the line of her throat.

This was really going to happen. She was going to have sex with Ethan. She was going to actually live out her fantasies.

And then it ended with a screech.

Breaking apart, they stared at each other while they struggled for breath. Ethan looked down at her and his expression told Sadie he was as stunned as she felt. Even in her wildest imaginings, Sadie had never expected to react to him as she had. It wasn't like she was a vestal virgin or something, either. She'd had sex. Plenty of times. But even the best of those nights couldn't hold a candle to what she felt when Ethan kissed her.

Then the baby cried again, that shriek coming through the baby monitor on the counter. Emma was demanding attention and there would be no ignoring her.

"I should go check on her," Sadie said brokenly.

"Yeah. Yeah, we should." Ethan let her go and took a step back.

Sadie had never felt colder in her life. Strange how the heat enveloping her dissipated instantly the moment she wasn't being held against him.

And strange that she didn't know whether to be

disappointed or grateful that the baby had interrupted them.

Hot sex, sure. But now that her blood was cooling off, she could think about the possible pitfalls of this. He'd paid her to stay for another month. If they were having sex all month—and didn't *that* sound great—would it be too weird? Did she care? And that was why she should be grateful, Sadie told herself. Her brain was confused enough already.

Little Emma had unwittingly given Ethan and Sadie more time to think. To look at every angle of what might happen and really decide if this was what they wanted—oh boy, she really wanted it. And she hoped he did, too.

"Okay, we'll…"

"Talk about this," he finished for her.

Nodding, she walked out of the kitchen, headed for the stairs and Emma. Ethan was right behind her and she was almost surprised that he was willing to do his part in taking care of the baby.

But a bigger part of her was wondering if their "talk" would turn into something else.

A few days later, they were already settling into a "routine." One that Ethan had never wanted. Having an infant in his house was unsettling enough, but seeing Sadie every day and every night was harder to deal with than he'd imagined. He'd been thinking about that kiss for days. Wanting more, knowing he shouldn't have it.

And still, he knew exactly what he wanted.

Sadie.

Funny how a few days could change everything. And this was one change he could completely get behind. Sadie was living in his house, in the room across from his. He'd tasted her and hadn't been able to sleep since for thinking about it. About *her*.

Neither of them had talked about it since, but the tension was there and building. Need pumped through him with a vengeance almost constantly, and damn it, it showed no signs of fading away. If anything, his desire for her had only grown since that one seductive kiss.

Five years. Five years he'd worked with her, known her and had never guessed what he might find if he kissed her. Just as well, he told himself. If he'd had any idea at all, he would have fired her years ago and seduced her on the spot.

Shaking his head, he tried to turn his mind back to work, but it was surprising how little the Mother's Day marketing campaign interested him at the moment. "Which is why you need to concentrate on it."

There were too many damn distractions in his life right now. They'd interviewed two would-be house-keepers and neither of them were right for the job. He and Sadie were bringing Emma to the in-house day care every day, but that couldn't keep going on.

Ethan wasn't going to be driving a child back and forth to work every morning and evening. He needed space. Time to think. He needed his life to get back into order.

As much as he wanted Sadie, as much as he wanted this day to be over and the two of them alone together back at the house, Ethan knew that being with her would open up all kinds of problems. What if she took sex the wrong way? What if she expected a relationship? What if she started looking at the two of them plus the baby as a family? No, he wasn't going down that road again.

He'd tried marriage once, completely screwed it up and had learned his lesson. He was no good at it. He liked his space and wasn't interested in being seen at the "best" parties, either. His ex-wife had made it plain when she walked out that he was less-than-stellar husband material.

When they married, Marcy had thought marrying a billionaire would mean great trips, big parties, celebrity friends. But that wasn't Ethan, and she hadn't bothered to hide her disappointment. He hadn't fought the divorce. What would have been the point? Marcy had been unhappy, so why try to keep her where she didn't want to be?

Besides, that brief marriage had taught Ethan an important lesson. He was better off on his own. He didn't like failure and so had no plans to set himself up for another disaster. He liked women, but he didn't want one permanently. Not even one who could make him feel what Sadie had.

As much as he burned to have her—under him, over him; didn't matter, he wasn't picky—he'd seen Sadie's eyes when she looked at the baby. When she held Emma, Sadie got a soft look about her, as if she were wrapping herself emotionally around that child. She clearly wanted kids. A marriage. A family.

What he wanted could be solved in a few hot, steamy nights.

"That does it," he muttered, and lunged out of his chair. He couldn't keep thinking about this. About *her*. It would drive him even crazier than he was feeling at the moment. Walking to the bank of windows behind his desk, he stared out at the ocean, hoping the view would ease the knots tightening inside him. He pushed one hand through his hair and wasn't the least bit surprised when Sadie's image rose to the front of his mind again.

When someone knocked, then opened his office door, he didn't bother to turn around.

"Ethan?"

He closed his eyes briefly. Even the sound of her voice now hit him with a visceral punch. "What is it, Sadie?"

"I just wanted to bring you the Donatello file. The meeting's in an hour, so..."

He glanced at her over his shoulder.

She shrugged and walked toward his desk. She

dropped the file on top, then said, "You know, I stopped by here that first night to pick up the file, thinking we could review it before the meeting... Then it got postponed again and I just forgot about it. Well, to be honest, I forgot about it that night. At the house. When we..."

He knew why, too. Hell, looking at her right now, he'd come up blank if anyone asked him anything about business. His gaze locked on hers and he felt a quick jolt of white-hot need that shot from his suddenly tight throat down to his groin, where it flashed into fire that felt as if it would consume him.

"Guess we both forgot things that night."

"And we haven't talked about why, yet."

He laughed shortly. "You really think *talking* is going to solve this?"

"I didn't know anything needed solving."

"Sadie..." He took a breath, blew it out and said, "You know damn well that what happened that night changed things."

"I do." She bit her lip and he flinched.

But he didn't want to talk. He wanted to taste. To touch. To explore. So he turned back to his desk, glanced at the file and added, "Thanks. I'll look it over before the meeting."

"Sure." She didn't leave.

"Is there something else?"

"Yes." She walked closer to the desk and stood opposite him. "What's going on?"

"I don't know what you mean." Yes, he did.

"Yes you do." She was wearing black slacks, a white shirt and a short red jacket that managed to draw his attention straight to her breasts. He'd almost had his hands on them last night and his palms itched to do it right now.

"Just leave it alone, Sadie," he ground out through gritted teeth. "This isn't the time."

"I don't think so. We said we'd talk. It's been days. It's past time. And I'm ready to talk."

"Here?"

"It's where we always are, Ethan," she pointed out.

"We can talk at the house tonight."

"Tonight we'll have the baby to take care of. At the moment, Emma's in day care, so we don't have any interruptions."

She folded her arms across her chest, lifting her breasts even higher, and Ethan wondered if she was doing it on purpose just to keep him off his game.

"Fine." He came around the desk, then perched on the edge of it so that they were nearly eye to eye. "Talk."

"Okay," she started, letting her arms fall to her sides. "I've done some thinking the last few nights. Actually, I did a *lot* of thinking."

"Me, too." Especially since he hadn't been able to sleep. Sadie's image had kept rising up in his mind. Her taste had lingered in his mouth, flavoring every breath.

"Good. I think that's good." She looked not nervous, but as if she were searching for every word. "So what I need to know is if you're thinking what I'm thinking."

"Which is?" He held his breath. If she said no to sex, he wasn't going back to the house. How the hell could he live across the hall from her and *not* have her?

"It's probably a really bad idea for us to sleep together."

"Wasn't thinking at all about *sleeping*," he told her.

"Yeah, me, either." She took a breath, licked her bottom lip and unknowingly sent arrows of heat darting through him. "But—"

There was a "but."

"—it's probably not a good idea," she said.

"Yeah." His chest felt tight. "That's what I think, too."

"Oh." She looked disappointed. "But the thing is, I also think we should do it, anyway."

He came off the desk in a blink, had her wrapped up in his arms and pressed along the length of him in seconds. "I agree," he said, then took her mouth with all the hunger that had haunted him through what felt like forever.

It was just like the first time. Ethan half expected to see actual flames licking up his body. He'd never known this flash-fire need before. Ethan had tried to tell himself that his reaction to Sadie was simply because it had been too long since he was with a woman. Any woman. He devoted so much of himself to work, there was rarely time to think about anything else.

But the truth was it was Sadie doing this to him. He'd never experienced such a mindless rush of desire before. Ethan wanted to believe his hunger for her would be eased by having her, but something told him it was only going to build. He didn't care.

Tasting her, stroking his tongue against hers, feeling her breasts crushed against his chest… This was all about *Sadie*. And beyond satisfying what he was feeling at the moment, he didn't want to think about what that might mean.

He couldn't touch her enough. Feel her enough. Her mouth joined to his, her tongue stroked his and Ethan felt those flames rising, growing more powerful. He had to have her. Her hands swept up his back to his shoulders, where her fingers curled in and held on. That simple action went straight to his groin and tightened his erection to the point of pain. Desire pumped wildly through his system, shutting down all thought beyond this moment. This had never happened to Ethan before. This complete loss of control. All he could think about was getting his hands on her.

With that thought in mind, he tore his mouth free

of hers, looked down and quickly opened that bright red jacket. Then the buttons on her shirt.

"Ethan…"

"Have to feel you under my hands," he murmured.

"Oh, good…"

He gave her a quick grin, pleased that she was as torn up as he was. Relieved that she hadn't said "stop." Stopping now might kill him. Ethan spread the fabric of her shirt apart and looked at her pale pink bra. "Pretty. But in my way."

"It unhooks in the front."

"Good news." He flicked the hook and eye open and her beautiful breasts spilled into his waiting hands. At the first touch of his skin to hers, she inhaled sharply. His thumbs and fingers worked her nipples as they jumped into life, going rigid with the need swamping her.

Ethan watched her eyes glaze over as he tugged on those twin sensitive points. He felt her reaction as if it were his own. She rocked her hips helplessly against him and he smiled again. Desire was alive and burning in the room, heat swirling around them like hot air from a blast furnace.

He did a quick turn, lifted Sadie and plopped her on the desk, then bent his head and took first one nipple, then the other into his mouth. Her taste filled him, her scent surrounded him and his mind was a fog from the physical demands crowding his body.

"Ethan…" Her voice was a strained whisper as

she threaded her fingers through his hair, her short, neat nails scraping along his scalp. He licked and nibbled and suckled at her breasts, drawing her deep into his mouth as the rush of heat building between them became all encompassing.

This. This was what he'd needed. To indulge himself in her. For years, he'd fought to ignore her, to bury his desire for her, until now it felt as if he were breaking free from the chains he'd wrapped around himself.

"Ethan," she choked out, "whatever you do, don't stop."

"Not the plan," he answered in a murmur. Again and again, he drew on her breasts, his mouth working her tender skin until she was writhing on the desk, helpless against the rising tension inside her. And he knew what he could do to help that.

He dropped one hand to the junction of her thighs and cupped her. At his first touch, she gasped, threw her head back and moved into him. Her slacks were in his way… That was all he could think. He wanted to touch her heat. Push his fingers inside and stroke her until he felt her climax pump through her.

But he couldn't stop long enough to give either of them that gift. For now, he stroked and rubbed and tasted and nibbled until she was a writhing mass of desire. Her response fueled his own. They both fought for air as the most basic of needs overtook everything else.

The first ripples of release hit her and Sadie leaned forward, burying her face in his shoulder. He heard the harsh, keening sound she made, but he knew she'd muffled it purposely so no one else in the building would guess what was happening here. Finally, she stopped, and Ethan took a breath and straightened up. Pulling away from her, he stepped back. Her eyes tracked him as she fought for air.

"What're you doing?"

"I'll be right back," he ground out, and congratulated himself silently on being able to speak at all.

"You're *leaving*?" She sounded outraged and he couldn't blame her. Hell, he could barely move for the pain in his hard, aching groin.

"No." He walked across the office, flipped the lock on the door and came back to her in a blink. "I'm making sure no one's going to walk in before we're finished."

"Oh, good. We're not finished."

"Not even close."

She nodded, licked her lips and sent a jolt of electricity to his dick. "Then locking the door was a good idea."

"I thought so." He walked to the other side of his desk, pulled open a middle drawer and took out the box of condoms he'd bought that morning when they'd stopped to get more diapers for Emma. Sadie was still watching him, and this time, she smiled. "I love a man who's prepared for any situation."

He disregarded the *L* word and went with what they were both feeling. "I bought these today. In case we actually did what we were working up to."

"Good call."

"But I don't want to wait until tonight." It cost him, this fight for control. His voice was thin, strained as he looked at her.

Her curls tumbled around her face. Her breasts were displayed in all their glory and her delicious lips parted as she slowly, deliberately, licked them again. This time, he could see, in anticipation.

"Neither do I." She scooted off the edge of the desk and shrugged her shirt and bra off. "Now, Ethan. We can talk later, but right now, I need you inside me before I explode."

"It's *when* I'm inside you that you're going to explode."

"Show me."

He tore the box, grabbed a condom and ripped the foil package open.

"Let me help," she whispered, holding out one hand for the sheer latex covering.

He moved in closer and handed it to her. Her nimble fingers undid his slacks, pulled the zipper down, then reached into his shorts to free him.

The minute her fingers curled around him, Ethan groaned. *Too long*, he told himself. It had been too long. Instantly, he realized that he was doing it again. Trying to explain away what he felt with Sadie by dismissing it. The truth was, he'd *never* reacted like this to a simple touch. Sadie's fingers curled around his length and stroked him slowly in a tantalizing motion that had him reaching for the ragged ends of his control.

Her thumb traced the tip of him, wiping away a single bead of moisture before sliding that, too, along the length of him. Her gaze was locked on his, so he saw the flash of desire burning in her eyes. Felt a similar burn within himself. "Put it on me, Sadie. I can't hold out much longer…"

She smiled at his admission and he saw that powerful look all women got when a man was at their mercy cross her features. Then it was gone and there was only desire again. She smoothed the condom down his length, making sure her fingers did another long tease of him as she did. By the time she was finished, Ethan was breathing hard and aching in every inch of his body. Need was a pulsing beast crouched inside him. And Ethan was done holding it back.

"That's it," he said, in what was more a growl of frustration than a simple statement. He undid her slacks and pushed them and her pale pink panties down her legs. She kicked them and her shoes off.

Then he dropped one hand to her hot, damp core again and she trembled, groaning out his name. One finger, then two, slid inside her, stroking, rubbing, exploring. His thumb smoothed across her core and she jolted in his arms, spreading her legs farther apart to accommodate him.

Ethan stared into her eyes, watching emotions flash and burn one after the other as she rocked her hips into his hand wildly. Then she came again in a sudden, hot rush of satisfaction. She bit down hard on her bottom lip to keep from crying out—still keeping quiet to protect them both from discovery.

He admired her control, but he wanted to break it. Wanted to hear her crying out his name, screaming it. He wanted—needed—more.

When the last of the tremors died away, Ethan reached out and swept everything off his desk to fly out and land on the hand-tied rug that lay across the wooden floor. Then he turned her around, laid her out across his desk and whispered, "Hold on."

He looked at her like she was a feast laid out before a starving man. And that was how it felt. Sunlight poured through the wall of windows and made her skin seem to glow. Ethan kept his gaze locked on her as he stripped his own clothes off and tossed them aside.

She curled her fingers around the edge of the desk, glanced back over her shoulder at him and parted her thighs. Then she whispered, "I'm ready, Ethan. I mean, *really* ready."

So was he. Ethan filled his gaze with her. Her bare butt was beautiful and waiting for him. He rubbed her behind hard, squeezing her flesh until she moaned and twisted her hips in response. She threw him a hot look and muttered, "Ethan, *now.*"

"Now," he agreed, and pushed his body home. In one long stroke, he was buried deep inside her heat. Her body moved and rocked to accommodate him and Ethan groaned at the satisfaction rippling through him.

He lost himself in the rush of finally joining with her. Of feeling her take him in. Her hips moved as her breath crashed in and out of her lungs. He couldn't stop looking at her. Looking at *them*, together.

Heart racing, Ethan felt her response, deep inside as her muscles contracted around him. Her climax hit hard and Sadie bit down on her lip again to keep from crying out. But he'd seen her reaction. Knew what they were doing to each other, and a moment later, Ethan gritted his teeth to muffle the sounds of his own surrender as he gave himself up to her.

A few minutes—or hours—later, when his heartbeat stopped thundering in his ears, Ethan was stunned at what they'd just done. Hell, he'd *never* had sex in his office before. Five minutes alone with Sadie and that record was smashed. Hell, he didn't know how he'd ever get any work done in here again. He would forever be seeing her stretched across his desk, deliciously naked.

Shaking his head, he carefully stepped back from Sadie, then helped her up. She moaned a little as she stood, and Ethan winced. "Damn it, Sadie, did I hurt you?"

She threw those blond curls out of her eyes and looked up at him with a wide grin. "Are you kidding? I feel fantastic!"

Just like that, he wanted her again. How had he not guessed all these years what kind of woman Sadie Matthews was? He'd thought of her as efficient and she was. But she was so much more, too.

This was going to be trouble.

She scrambled to get back into her clothes, so Ethan did the same. Once they were dressed, though, he took hold of her shoulders. "That was crazy."

"I know," she said, still giving him that wide smile. "Honestly, it was crazy *and* amazing."

He scrubbed one hand across the back of his neck and watched her. "That talk we were supposed to have? I think it's time we had it."

"Okay." She stared up into his eyes and Ethan's mind went blank for a long second or two. Hell, he'd completely lost focus. Another first.

All he could think about was what had just happened between them and how badly he wanted to do it again.

"You start," she said, and walked around him. She squatted down to pick up the scattered papers and pens he'd pushed off his desk.

Irritated somehow, Ethan snapped, "You don't have to do that."

She glanced up at him. "I do still work here, Ethan. Relax."

His brain was racing and she was telling him to relax. Not going to happen. When she'd gathered everything, he reached down for her arm and helped her up. She set it all down on the desk, then gave the wood a soft pat.

"I'm going to have real affection for this desk from now on."

He didn't know what to make of her. They'd worked together closely for five years and Ethan felt like he didn't know her at all. She wasn't horrified or regretful or even embarrassed. She reveled in what had happened between them and Ethan envied that. Because he wasn't at all sure they hadn't made a huge mistake. He really hated this uncertain feeling. Ethan always knew what to do, what to say, in any given situation. This off-balance sensation was unsettling.

"You're still worried and you don't have to be," she said softly. Walking up to him, she laid one hand on his chest and looked up into his eyes. "What happened here is because we both wanted it to happen. You don't owe me anything and I'm not asking for anything, so you can get that slightly panicked look off your face."

Offended somehow, he instantly smoothed out his features. "I'm not panicked. I just don't want you to think that this means more than what it was."

Now she laughed shortly and gave his chest a pat.

"Ethan, I've known you for five years. If anyone knows you're not a relationship person, it's *me*. Besides, I quit, remember?" She threaded her fingers through her curls, then said, "In four weeks, I'll be gone and you won't have to worry about any of this."

Then she walked across the room and opened the door. Giving him a finger wave, she slipped through and he was alone again. The room was still humming with sexual energy and all Ethan could think about was what she'd said.

In four weeks, I'll be gone.

And damn it, he already knew that four weeks wouldn't be enough.

Six

Gabriel had it all worked out.

A chef at Heart Chocolates would be making the samples of the new flavors. This was the best idea all around. Not only did Jeff Garret already work for him as an assistant chocolate chef, he was looking to advance his career. Plus, Gabriel didn't have to take the recipe out of the company fold. A win—win. All he had to do was find a professional kitchen he could rent for a couple nights.

"I still don't understand why you didn't use the chef I arranged," Pam said, anger clear in her tone.

And Gabe didn't understand why she was so pissed. But she had been ever since he'd told her the new plan. "Because I don't know him."

"I do," she argued.

"That's great," Gabe said, "but Jeff's a chef with my company. He's studied with the top chocolatier in Belgium and he wants more responsibility at the company. This is his chance to prove himself." Gabe stopped, laughed a little and said, "I guess Jeff and I have a lot in common in this."

She scowled at him. "This isn't funny, Gabe. Not to me."

"Yeah, I can see that." He studied her for a second or two. "What I don't know is *why*?"

She shook her head, obviously thinking about it briefly, and said, "We were doing this together, and now all of a sudden we're not. What am I supposed to tell my friend?"

Now she was concerned that her chef friend would have his feelings hurt? His professional pride? Well, that really wasn't one of Gabe's big concerns.

"Tell him the truth," Gabe countered. "That this is my family's recipe and I can't trust it to just anyone."

"I'm 'just anyone'? Good to know." Pam whirled away so fast her long dark hair swung out around her shoulders like a cape. Then she spun back to look up at him. "You weren't trusting my chef, Gabe. You were supposed to be trusting *me*."

She turned again and this time walked away from him.

Gabe caught up with her quickly. Grabbing her

arm, he whirled her around and looked down into her big brown eyes. "I do trust you."

"Sure." Her gaze slid from his. "I'm convinced."

He was getting more confused by the minute. Ever since he'd told her about using one of the Heart chefs, she'd been irritated and hadn't bothered to hide it.

They were in his penthouse apartment at the hotel. They were supposed to be celebrating with a great dinner and an icy cold bottle of champagne he'd ordered from one of the best restaurants in the city. But the dinner was uneaten and the champagne was rapidly going flat.

This was not how Gabe had thought the evening would go. He'd planned the great dinner and then figured on having some celebrational sex when they were finished. Looked like that was out the window.

When Pam stormed through the living room and out onto the balcony overlooking the ocean, Gabe followed her. This was the first time he'd ever seen her temper. And though it was impressive, he also found it sexy as hell. He liked a woman with fire in her eyes. He'd just like to know what had caused all this.

"I don't understand why you didn't stick to the plan," she said.

"Because this plan's better. I told you. This way the family recipe stays in the family." He looked at her, and even in profile he could see the suppressed anger on her face. Well, he wasn't too far behind her on that front.

"I'm sorry," she said suddenly and just like that, his own temper drained away. "I was just surprised, Gabe. You didn't even tell me you were changing the plan."

"Hey." He took her arm, turned her around to face him. "Honestly, I didn't think it would bug you so much. This isn't about trust, Pam."

"Isn't it?" She pulled free of his grasp and took a step back. Holding on to the wrought-iron railing with one hand, she pushed her windblown hair out of her eyes with the other.

He threw both hands high in exasperation. How did this go sideways so fast? "We're a team, Pam. Nothing has changed."

"Doesn't feel like it." She shook her head. "Not anymore."

"What the hell, Pam?" He shoved his hands into his jeans pockets. "Where's all the fury coming from? I don't know your chef from a hole in the ground. Why wouldn't I use one I already know? The guy's insanely talented. And he already works for me."

"Fine." She waved a hand at him, effectively dismissing that argument. "But now I have to explain to my chef why he can't be in on the ground floor of a new chocolate line."

"He wouldn't have been, anyway," Gabe argued. "He was going to make samples. That's as far as his involvement went. But if this goes well, then Jeff will get a promotion and I'll have the satisfaction of hearing Ethan apologize and admit he was wrong for the first damn time ever."

She didn't look like she cared much.

"This is making zero sense," Gabe said, his own frustration building. "And damned if I'm going to apologize for protecting my family even while I'm sneaking around behind their backs."

"Hey," she said quickly. "Nobody's *forcing* you to do anything. You *wanted* to do this," she reminded him. "I didn't talk you into it. In fact, I told you that you didn't *have* to do it at all."

He stepped up closer, laid both hands on her shoulders and could practically feel her vibrating with anger. The woman was making him crazy. "Babe, I know that. This whole thing is on me. Which is why I'm doing it my way. You said you understood family loyalty."

"I do."

"Then you should get why I'm doing it like this."

She considered that, then took a breath and huffed it out again. "I get it, Gabe. I just don't know why you kept it from me."

"I only finalized it today," he argued. "Hell, I didn't see you until a half hour ago. When was I going to tell you?"

"When you started thinking about changing the plan?"

There was more going on here than anger over a

plan changing. Something else was bugging her. He just had no idea what it was. "What's really going on here, Pam?"

Below, the ocean was dark, but the waves were topped with froth that stood out in the moonlight. Couples strolled the sand at the water's edge and a few bonfires winked in the blackness of the beach.

"What do you mean?"

"This is about more than using a different chef," he said, as suspicion slipped through his mind. He didn't like the feeling. But what the hell else was he supposed to think when her reaction to all of this was so damn irrational?

Pam was the one he could count on. Talk to. She'd been his sounding board for months. Always supportive. Always ready to listen. If something had changed, he wanted to know what it was. "So tell me what's happening."

"There's nothing to tell," she said, then pulled her phone from her back pocket to check the time. "I've got to go. It's my father's birthday and the whole family's gathering at their house."

"You didn't say anything before."

"Well, I am now," she murmured.

"But we've got dinner. Champagne."

"Yeah, I don't feel much like celebrating."

She slipped out of his grasp and his hands felt empty, cold. "Damn it, Pam, tell me what's going on with you."

"It's nothing."

Before he could say anything else, she was walking back into the main room and snatching her purse up off the couch. The table, set for an intimate dinner, complete with candles, was ignored. "Pam."

She stopped, turned and looked at him. In her eyes he could see disappointment still shining there. Her mouth was tight and flat, and her spine was stiff. "What?"

He didn't know what had gone wrong here, so he didn't know how to fix it. That was an irritation, too. Looking at her now, he could see that though she was standing right there, she was miles away emotionally. But until she was willing to talk to him about what was bothering her there wasn't a hell of a lot he could do about it.

"Are you going to be there when we make the new chocolates?"

Her mouth curved though her eyes remained the same—dark, closed off. "Of course I will. I want to see this through with you."

"Good," he said. "I'll call you tomorrow."

"Sure, Gabe. Tomorrow." Then she left and he wondered if this idea was going to ruin his and Pam's relationship as surely as it would his and Ethan's.

"They're holding out for more money." Ethan sat back in his desk chair a few days later and looked up at Sadie.

Her breath caught in her throat. Not so long ago, she'd been sprawled across that desk like the main course at a feast. And the memory of it sent a quick ripple of excitement along her spine. Hard to keep your mind on work when all you could think about was...

"Sadie? Are you listening?"

"What?" She snapped back. "Yes. Of course. They want more money."

"I thought we were close to finalizing. The old man, he wants to sell, but his adult children are making him have second thoughts." Ethan tossed a pen onto his desktop and pushed himself to his feet. "The lawyers, ours and theirs, are trying to hammer out a deal, but—"

"Why don't you do it personally?" Sadie asked.

He shifted to look at her. "I don't do the negotiating. That's why I pay the lawyers."

She chuckled and shook her head. "That's the way we usually do it, yes. But Donatello's might be different."

"How?"

He'd tucked the edges of his suit jacket back and had his hands tucked into his pockets. He looked the epitome of the high-powered businessman. And yet, looking at him, she could see him as he was when they were together, and that sent heat waves rocketing through her body.

"Sadie?"

Wow, she really had to concentrate. "Okay, um, I mean that Donatello's is a family business."

"Yeah, I know. I just told you. It's the kids who are fighting this buyout. They're the ones demanding more money, and at the same time, telling their father not to sell at all." He scowled fiercely. "If they'd just butt out, we could have this done. I don't know why they're being so difficult, anyway. We're offering a fair price."

Funny that he couldn't see the similarities between the Hart family and the Donatello family. Richard Donatello's adult children were fighting for their legacy, their own family's traditions, just as Ethan was. As important as the chocolate company was to him, he should understand what the Donatello kids were going through.

"Right." Sadie shrugged. "Well, you know how you feel about the Hart family business. We both know you would do whatever it took to keep this company thriving. So just for a minute, put yourself in their place."

He snorted. "Not the same. Not by a long shot. Yes, Donatello's has a great reputation, but they're still a small, one-shop business."

"Just how Heart Chocolates started."

"A long time ago," he pointed out.

Honestly, sometimes Sadie felt like beating her own head against a brick wall. It would certainly be more satisfying than trying to convince Ethan that he was wrong about *anything*.

"Donatello's has been around for almost fifty years."

He frowned.

"And it's successful enough that you want to buy it."

"Well, yes," he argued. "Because they have a great web presence, an excellent location in Laguna and their customer list is phenomenal."

"All good points," she said, wondering why he still wasn't getting it. Really, was it possible that once you reached success, you actually *forgot* how it had happened? "What I'm saying is that the Donatello chocolate shop is where yours started out a hundred years ago. Hardworking. A family. Building a reputation."

He frowned again, but she could see that he was considering what she was saying. It was a start, Sadie told herself, so she went on.

"Is offering him more money such a horrible thing?" she asked. "Hasn't he earned it? Richard Donatello built a company that you badly want. Maybe if the kids see that you treated their father well, they'll back off."

"Maybe." He nodded thoughtfully.

"And think about it, Ethan…you paid me an extra hundred and fifty thousand for one month."

"Yeah," he said tightly, "that was personal. This is business."

He had the wide windows behind him, where gray, January clouds scuttled across the horizon, hovering over a sea the color of steel.

"Not completely," she argued, and watched one of his eyebrows arch. "Business, sure. But it's also about family. Their family, Ethan. A legacy as important to them as yours is to you."

A couple long, tense seconds passed before he nodded again. "All right. You've made your point. I'll give it some thought."

Sadie knew when to leave well enough alone. "Okay, good. Now back to the personal front—"

"I don't have time for a quickie today, Sadie."

She blinked and her head jerked back as if she'd been slapped. Staring at him, she could see that he wished he hadn't said that, but it was enough to know that he was thinking it. "I don't remember asking for one."

"No, you didn't." He sighed, shook his head and rubbed the back of his neck. "I'm sorry. That didn't come out right."

"Oh, I don't know. You made yourself pretty clear," she said stiffly. And she'd really love to know what had brought on such an insult to her—to both of them. What they'd shared had been far more than a "quickie." There'd been emotions involved as well as their bodies, but apparently, Ethan didn't want to admit that to her or himself. "As it happens, I wasn't talking about sex, Ethan. I was going to tell you the agency is sending over another housekeeper to be interviewed tonight."

"Oh." He frowned. "Fine."

Apparently he was going to pretend he didn't say anything, and she was supposed to pretend she hadn't heard it. Well, fine. She could do avoidance and pretense as well as anyone. Hadn't she been hiding her love for this idiot man for five long years?

"Her name is Julie Cochran. She's a single mother of a five-year-old. She's a good cook, has no issues with also looking after a baby, and she really needs the job."

His jaw dropped and his eyes went wide. "You want to move *another* child into my house?"

Sadie almost sighed. She'd really thought they'd been making progress over the last few days. Hearing him now was more than disappointing. "I'm sure the little girl doesn't have the plague or anything, so you should be safe."

"That's not funny."

"No," she agreed. "None of this is funny. But Julie is a single mom who needs work. The agency says she's one of their best—"

"Then why is she out of work?"

"Because the woman she worked for was elderly and recently died."

He frowned. "Oh."

"Ethan, you want someone good with kids. Well, Julie is. The housekeeper's quarters are big enough

for her and her daughter, *and* she's a cook, as well."
She shouldn't have to work so hard to sell him on
this. "She pretty much hits every point you needed."

"I didn't need another child," Ethan ground out.
"Hell, I didn't want the one I've got."

"Wow." Sadie just stared at him. For some reason,
she'd thought he was coming around a little. He was
helping take care of Emma. He'd fed her and bathed
her the night before. The two of them together had
tucked the baby in for the night. So what was the
problem?

"Damn it, don't look at me like that."

"How?" she asked. "Horrified? Disappointed?"

"Either," he muttered. "Both."

"I don't know who I'm more insulted for," she admitted. "Me or Emma."

"I'm not trying to insult either one of you."

"Well, congratulations then," she said tightly.
"You appear to be so gifted with insults you don't
need to try."

"Damn it, Sadie—"

"I'm not talking about me now, Ethan. This is
about Emma. You've only had her a little more than
a week," she said, reminding herself as well as him
of that fact. Maybe he'd need more time to get used
to having Emma in his house. But what kind of ex-
cuse was she supposed to make to cover the insult
he'd delivered to *her*? "Give it a chance."

"I am, aren't I?"

"Are you?" she countered. "Honestly, I thought you were. You're really good with Emma, but hearing you now, I don't know if you're doing the right thing in keeping her."

He stared at her, surprised. "What else can I do? I promised her father I'd be her guardian."

"A guardian is more than a place to live and a housekeeper to make sure the child is fed and clean." Sadie stared him down. "A decade-old promise isn't enough reason to keep her, Ethan. Emma needs more than your duty. Heck, she *deserves* more than that. She deserves to be loved. If you can't do that, maybe you should consider giving her up for adoption to someone who can."

Now he looked stunned. "You really think I'd do that?"

"Before the last five minutes, no," she admitted. "But listening to you complain is pretty convincing."

"That's great. Thanks." He paced behind his desk and she thought he looked like a tiger in a too-small cage. "Good to know I have your support."

"Like I have yours?" she countered just as hotly. "What was that you said about a *quickie*?"

He stopped pacing and threw her a look that was both apologetic and irritated. Amazing that he could conflate the two. "You know damn well I didn't mean anything by that."

"Do I?"

"You sure as hell should," he snapped. "We've

known each other too long for you to take one stupid comment and build a case on it."

There was more going on here than just the baby and the housekeeper and the constant change in a life that had been so rooted in routine that it was more of a rut than a path forward. And maybe it was time he told her what was bothering him.

"What's going on with you, Ethan?" she asked quietly.

"Nothing."

"Right." She crossed her arms over her chest. "You've barely spoken to me since we were together. You leave every morning without a word, and when you are forced to talk to me at work, you're cold and distant. And let's just add, as of today, insulting."

"I said I was sorry."

"Well, all better then." She uncrossed her arms, then set her hands at her hips. "Why are you avoiding me?"

"I've been busy."

"Hey, me, too," she said, walking toward him. "And I'm also the one who took Emma to the day care. The one who checked on her at lunch, and I'm guessing I will be the one driving her back to the house. You've been ignoring both of us, Ethan. Why?"

He glared at her, then looked away. "Because things are different since we had sex."

Surprised, she asked, "Different how?"

He snapped her a look. "Hell, it changed every-thing. I've thought about it and realized that what we did was a mistake."

Sadie flushed and felt both rage and embarrass-ment rise up inside her. Strange, she hadn't been embarrassed at all while she was laid out in front of him. But hearing him dismiss what they'd shared was enough to color her own memories of it. "Is that right?"

"It is," he said tightly, and locked his gaze on hers. "There's too much going on right now and I don't think we should let that happen again."

"How long have you been working on that speech?"

"What?"

Sadie was furious. This was why he'd been ignor-ing her? He had regrets over what they'd done, and like the lord of the manor, he was going to put every-thing right again. Men were just idiots sometimes. He thought insulting her, ignoring her, would be enough to keep her at a distance. Clearly, he didn't know her as well as he thought he did.

"*You* don't think," she said, keeping her voice as calm as possible. "You've decided. Thank you, Ethan. How very kind of you to figure all of this out without any input from me."

He winced a little. "If you'll just listen…"

"Now you're ready to talk and I should just, what? Sit down and listen as you lay out your plans?"

"I didn't say that…"

"Let me ask you, Ethan, do I get a vote in any of this?"

"Of course you get a vote," he practically snarled, and came to a stop behind his desk, as if he needed that heavy piece of mahogany furniture as a barrier between them.

But only a few days ago it had been so much more than that.

"Well, that's very democratic of you, Ethan."

He frowned and watched her warily. "The words sound right, but the tone is off."

"Good catch," she said. "But the real question is, why didn't you talk to me about this before you made up your new rules?"

He scrubbed one hand across his jaw. "It's complicated."

"No, it isn't." Sadie was frustrated and her fury was beginning to ease back down into extreme irritation. "For heaven's sake, Ethan, it doesn't have to be complicated unless you make it so. Whatever you're thinking, just stop it."

He laughed shortly. "Sure. I'll stop thinking."

"You overthink, Ethan. That's the problem." Shaking her head, Sadie stepped forward, laid both hands on the edge of the desk and said, "We had each other, right here."

His eyes flashed.

"Why can't you just let it be what it was?" she asked. "Two adults enjoying each other."

"You said that then."

"And will again tomorrow if I have to," Sadie said, folding her arms across her chest again and giving him a hot stare. "And I probably will, because you don't seem to be listening. I didn't ask you for anything, Ethan, remember? You don't owe me anything and I don't need you to protect me from big bad you."

He reached up and shoved both hands through his hair. "I don't want this—whatever it is we've got going on here—getting messy."

"It will."

His head snapped up and his eyes fired.

She sighed. "Life gets messy, Ethan. It just happens. But relax. I won't be crawling at your feet, begging for scraps of attention."

"I never said you would," he said in his own defense.

"And you're perfectly safe from a proposal, too," Sadie reassured him. "Trust me when I say you are not the man for me."

He actually looked offended. "What's that supposed to mean?"

"It means," she told him, "that I have a list of qualifications for the man I want and you only meet one of them." She stopped, thought about the impromptu hot sex on the desk in the middle of the day and had to admit that he was not only *sexy*, but had proved himself to be *adventurous*, too. "Okay, two. But that's not enough."

"How many points are on this dubious list?" he asked, frowning.

"Five," she said. "And two out of five is not nearly good enough for me. So believe me when I say you're completely safe."

"Great." He was still frowning, and if anything, the offended expression on his features had deepened.

Not a bad thing, she told herself. Maybe it was good that Ethan find out he wasn't the prime catch he thought he was.

"So, if you're okay now, I'm going back to work." She turned for the door and stopped. "You will be at the house tonight to interview Julie?"

"Yeah."

"Good. And once you've completely recovered from this conversation, maybe we could try out a bed next time…"

She didn't wait to hear his answer.

She didn't need to.

She left and stood with her back to the closed door. The office was bustling, phones were ringing and fingers clacked on keyboards. But she wasn't paying attention to any of it.

Instead, her mind was on the man she would soon be walking away from. Forever.

Seven

"So what do you think?"

Ethan looked over at Sadie and saw the gleam of triumph in her eyes. He couldn't blame her. "I think you were right. Julie will work out."

"Wow. *I was right.* I like hearing that."

One of his eyebrows lifted. "Don't get used to it."

She laughed and, God, the sound of it slammed into the center of his chest and tightened everything inside him. After their conversation that afternoon, he would have bet every penny he had that Sadie would make him pay, by dishing out silence and cold, hard stares. It was how every other woman he'd ever known had gone about payback. About making sure he understood just how wrong he'd been in whatever personal situation was happening at the time.

He should have known that Sadie would be different here, too. She was behaving like they hadn't had an argument at all.

"I don't know," she said with a grin. "I think I'm on a roll. You're offering Donatello's more money. You hired Julie in spite of her little girl…"

True, he had upped his offer for the Laguna chocolate shop. He hadn't heard anything yet, but Sadie had made a good point that he hadn't thought about before. Donatello's was a small shop, but they'd been in their location for forty-five years. They'd built a family business just as his own family had. That was something to respect, and a part of Ethan was ashamed that until Sadie spoke up, he hadn't noticed. Hadn't *let* himself notice. And that admission was a hard one to make.

As for Julie, that had turned out to be the easiest damn decision he'd ever made. Yes, there was now *another* child in his house, but even Ethan had to admit, at least to himself, that Alli was a cute kid. Didn't mean he was getting soft. Only that he had eyes, he assured himself.

"It was her chicken dinner that sold me," he admitted.

"Can't blame you for that. It was delicious. Now you know why she insisted on cooking for us. To prove she knows her way around a kitchen." Sadie leaned back on the couch and propped her feet up on the low table in front of her. She had tiny feet. Why was that sexy? He shook his head to clear out distracting thoughts.

"Yeah," he said, remembering the dinner Julie had fixed for them. "Makes me wonder why I put up with Alice all those years."

"Because you hate change?"

He looked at her and caught the impish gleam in her eyes. "Must be it," he agreed. Though for a man who hated change as much as he did, there'd been plenty of it in his life lately.

Most of it revolving around the woman smiling at him. But then, so much of his life over the last five years had revolved around Sadie. She'd been a constant in his daily life. At work, which was really the only life he had, she was irreplaceable. And he was only just now figuring that out. So what did that say about him?

Frowning, he glanced around the empty room, then back to where Sadie was reclining on the deeply cushioned couch. Suddenly, he realized that they were alone in the house but for baby Emma. Julie and her daughter wouldn't be moving in until the following day.

And in spite of everything he'd said only that afternoon, he wanted Sadie so badly it was an ache inside him. To hell with rules. Plans. If she wanted him, too, why shouldn't they have each other again?

"So with Julie willing to watch Emma, I guess you don't really need me to stay the full month, right?"

Startled, he realized *that* hadn't occurred to him. The firelight streaming from the hearth danced across her features and shifted in shadows that seemed to settle in her blue eyes. Why hadn't he thought of that? He had almost three more weeks to go with Sadie and damn it, he wanted them.

He'd already wasted too much time, worried about consequences when she clearly wasn't.

"We still need to find a nanny," he said firmly.

"Yes, but Julie will be able to watch Emma until you do, so…"

Ethan pushed up off the far end of the leather sofa and walked over to her. Reaching down, he pulled her from the couch, and when she was standing right in front of him, he said, "Yeah, I paid you to stay a month. I still need you here."

"Why?" She looked up into his eyes and he found he couldn't look away.

He told her the honest truth. "Because I'm not ready for you to leave yet."

"Why?" She smiled and that simple curve of her mouth tugged at something inside him.

He gave her a reluctant smile. "Going to make me say it?"

She tipped her head to one side in that move he was so fond of, and said, "Yes. I think I am."

"Fine." He nodded, swallowed hard and let the desire pumping inside him have free rein. His body tightened; his heartbeat thundered in his chest. "You're right about this, too. I want you, Sadie. I want you all the damn time. Every time I have you it only makes me want more."

"And that's a good thing, right?" she asked, and made her only reference to what they'd talked about just that afternoon.

Best thing that had ever happened to him, not that Ethan was going to be admitting that anytime soon.

"It's a damn gift is what it is," he ground out.

She wrapped her arms around his neck and said, "Well, what're we standing here for?"

"Good question."

He swept her up into his arms and Sadie felt a bone-deep thrill rush through her. He held her close to his chest, looked down into her eyes, and she read the hunger shining there. Clearly, he was done trying to pretend that what was between them could be ignored or pushed aside. That hunger radiating from Ethan fed what she was feeling, making her tremble with reaction.

It had been days since they'd been together and Sadie had wondered if they ever would be again. She knew Ethan so well and had realized that over the last few days, he'd questioned himself, what had happened, and tried to work out every possibility, up to and including never touching her again. He was a man with a hard inner line that he didn't cross on a whim. But here he was, holding her, looking down at her with a promise of what was to come, and Sadie silently acknowledged that she still loved him. Would always love him. And it wouldn't matter if she left. Didn't matter if she tried to find someone else to make a life with.

A part of her would always be here. With Ethan.

"You accused me of overthinking, but I can see the wheels in your mind turning," he said as he walked toward the stairs. "Changing your mind?"

"Not at all." Caught, she scrambled for something to say that wouldn't give away what she was feeling. So she went with humor. "I was just wondering how quickly you could take the stairs…"

"We're about to find out," he said with a grin, and made it to the second floor in seconds.

"Impressive," she said, and dragged her nails against the back of his neck.

He inhaled sharply and turned toward the master bedroom. "I'm just getting started impressing you."

A sizzling knot of anticipation settled in the pit of her stomach and made her blood fizz like champagne. Reaching up, she stroked his cheek and he gritted his teeth in response.

There was no sound from the baby's room, thank goodness, because Sadie didn't want an interruption. Not even from the cutest baby in the world.

All she wanted now was Ethan. She would always want Ethan.

When he carried her into his bedroom, Sadie took a moment to look around. In all the time she'd known him, she'd never seen it before. Over the years, when she'd come to his house, it was for business, and she'd worked with him in his office downstairs or in the main room or even outside on the patio.

Now, it was personal, and she felt as if she were being given a glimpse into the man.

The room was massive, of course, as she'd expected for being in a mansion. There was a huge TV hanging on the wall opposite the bed. A wide bank of windows looked out over the backyard and the ocean beyond. She guessed that in daylight, the view would be gorgeous. Now, though, she saw only the dark with the pale wash of solar lights on the lawn.

Beneath the TV was a fireplace, cold now, and twin comfy chairs pulled up in front of it. There was a long, low dresser on another wall and tables on either side of a gigantic bed that was covered in a navy blue duvet and mounded with pillows in shades of blue and gray.

"It's nice," she said, and knew that sounded lame, but really, she'd been lucky to squeeze those two words out of her tight throat. The room was lovely, but impersonal. There were no hints to the inner thoughts of Ethan Hart. It was as if this were a palatial hotel room. And actually, that's what it was.

Though Ethan owned this beautiful home, until the last week or so, he'd spent almost no time in it. At most, it was a place to sleep and to store his clothes.

There were no family photos in the room, no scattered coins on the dresser or keys casually discarded. Sadie realized that outside of his office, his company, Ethan had less of a life than she'd guessed. But maybe she could help him change that while she was there.

"Thanks," he said, "glad you like it." He gave her a wry smile, walked to the bed and dropped her onto the mattress.

Sadie yelped in surprise, then grinned as she bounced. "Very suave."

"Again. Thanks."

She toed off her shoes and let them hit the floor with a thud. Then her fingers went to the buttons on her shirt. He was watching every move she made and Sadie loved the flash of heat she saw in his eyes.

"Trying to make me crazy by undoing those buttons extra slowly?"

"Is it working?" She knew it was. She could feel his impatience building as quickly as her own. It felt like forever since she'd touched him. Since he'd been inside her.

"Way too well," he said tightly, and tore off his own shirt, sending buttons skittering across the hardwood floor.

She drew in a fast, deep breath. He must have a

gym somewhere in this palace, Sadie told herself, because the man's body was sharply defined muscles that made her fingers itch to touch him. He undid his slacks, stepped out of them and his shorts, and then he was standing in front of her and her heartbeat jumped into a gallop. His chest wasn't the only impressive physical trait the man possessed.

"You're overdressed," he murmured, leaning forward to unhook her jeans and pull them down and off her legs. Then he gave her a smile of appreciation. "If I'd known you were wearing black lace, it might not have taken us so long to get here."

In the heat of his gaze, Sadie felt beautiful. Powerful. Her stomach swirled as she sat up, undid her shirt and shrugged it off to display the matching black lace bra.

"You are a picture," he whispered. "But you're still overdressed."

She smiled up at him. "Why don't you see what you can do about that?"

He reached for her and she rose up to meet him. His fingers flicked the clasp of her bra free and his eyes fired even as he filled his hands with her breasts and rubbed her pebbled nipples with his thumbs.

Sadie's head fell back as a buzz of awareness swirled through her, tightening into a coil in the pit of her stomach. It felt so good. *He* felt so good. His hands were strong and gentle and oh so talented.

She opened her eyes to look up at him and saw

her own desire reflected in his gaze. "I've missed you," she admitted.

"I missed you, too," he said softly, "and I didn't want to."

Sadie almost laughed. That was so Ethan. "Then it's twice as nice to hear," she said, and took his face in her palms to kiss him.

Instantly, he levered her back onto the bed and covered her body with his. His mouth latched on to hers and their tongues twisted together in a sensual dance that began slowly and in seconds became breathless, frenzied. Sadie ran her hands up and down his arms, up to his broad shoulders. She curled her fingers in, holding on to him as if to keep him right where he was. His hands swept up and down her body; his fingers hooked around the thin elastic of her panties and pushed them down. She lifted her hips, helping him. She wanted nothing between them, not even that tiny scrap of lace.

He dipped his head to her breast and Sadie took a harsh breath at the sensation of him drawing her body into his mouth. He suckled her, drawing and pulling until it felt as if he would tear her soul from her and into him. And while she sighed and writhed beneath him, he touched her core, dipping his fingers into her heat as he had once before, and this time it was even better.

Because they were here, in his house, and she could shout if she wanted to? Because she'd finally accepted that the love she felt for him wasn't going anywhere?

Did it matter why? No. All that mattered was his next kiss. The next touch. The next breathless anticipation. In the next instant, she pushed every thought aside. Nothing mattered but this moment. She wanted it to go on forever. The feeling of his body against hers. His hands on her skin.

"God, you smell good," he whispered, tracking his lips and tongue along her skin, up to her throat, where he nibbled at her pulse beat.

She tipped her head to one side to give him better access and slid her hands up and down his back. "And oh, you feel good."

He lifted his head, looked down at her and smiled. "I really do feel good, thanks."

She laughed and realized that until this time with him, she'd almost never seen his sense of humor. Sadie enjoyed this closeness between them. Beyond the sex, beyond their bodies coming together, this link was everything she'd ever hoped for. This easiness between them was worth everything.

The smiles, the laughter, the shared sighs and the breathless need all combined to make Sadie feel as if she and Ethan really were connecting on a much deeper level than simply physically.

He sat up and pulled away then, reaching for the bedside table. She knew what he was doing and she was all for it. "Hurry up, Ethan."

He shot her a grin. "We have all night, Sadie. No need to hurry."

All night. Didn't that sound wonderful? But for now, she had an ache demanding to be satisfied. She went up on her elbows and tossed her hair back out of her face. "Hurry now, take our time later."

He sheathed himself with a condom, turned back to her and said softly, "Yes, ma'am."

Grabbing hold of her butt, he pulled her closer, lifted her legs and draped them over his shoulders. Sadie shifted, writhed, wiggled her hips, anything she could do to entice him to get on with it. She felt as if she were wired so tightly she might just explode, and nobody wanted that.

Then she almost did, the moment his mouth covered her core. She was helpless in his grasp. All she could do was moan and shout and beg for the release he kept just out of reach. Sadie watched him, reached down and ran her fingers through his hair, then held him to her. He licked her, nibbled at her, scoring her center lightly with the edges of his teeth. Again and again, his tongue claimed her, stirring that one sensitive bud until it felt as if it were electrified.

She rocked her hips because it was the only move available to her. He took her higher, faster, than he had before, and Sadie fought for air. She didn't want to pass out and miss anything about this moment. She couldn't tear her gaze from him.

His hands kneaded her butt while his mouth tormented her. He didn't stop, not even when her climax erupted and turned her into a writhing, screaming mess, trying to hold on to the world so she wouldn't fall off.

Before the last ripple had coursed through her, Ethan dropped her to the mattress and claimed her body in one long, hard stroke. Sadie felt shattered. As if she'd come apart and now he was tormenting the jagged pieces. And she moved into him to make him go faster, deeper.

He set a rhythm designed to drive her insane. Caught, held in place by his strength, she lifted her hips, rocking high to take him deep. Sadie curled her fingers into the silky duvet and held on tight.

"Ethan!"

"Come on," he ordered harshly, his voice hardly more than a scrape of sound. "Come again, Sadie. Come for me."

She shook her head. If she climaxed again, she might never be put back together again. And yet there was no stopping it. She screamed his name again and relished the feeling of his body slamming into hers, over and over again.

She felt it coming, so she opened her eyes so she could look at him when he pushed her over the edge. His eyes burned as his gaze locked on her. He moved faster, harder, and Sadie rushed to meet that crashing release. And when it claimed her, she shouted his name like a prayer.

Once again, Ethan didn't give her body time to stop shaking, shivering, before he moved and changed the game again. Smoothly, he shifted to lay on his back, taking her with him. Sadie straddled him then and braced her hands on his hard, sculpted chest.

He was embedded so deeply inside her now, she wanted to savor that feeling, keep it with her always. His hands came down on her hips and Sadie smiled at him. "Your turn, Ethan."

She moved on him, and this time it was *her* setting the pace, her driving the action and creating a rhythm that drove Ethan to the edge of madness. She watched him, saw his eyes glaze with passion, felt the strength of his hands tighten on her hips. She swiveled on him, deepening their contact, driving them both now. Sadie knew another orgasm was coming and she held it back, wanting to reach that peak with Ethan this time.

And when he was ready, she took his surrender and gave him her own. Seconds, minutes, maybe hours ticked past as their bodies exploded in tandem. Then she crashed down onto his chest and was cradled in his arms.

"That was…" Sadie said with an exhausted, yet exhilarated sigh.

"Yeah, it was." Ethan dragged his hands up and

down her spine, keeping her right where she was, sprawled on top of him.

"I don't think I can move," she admitted. Never in her life had Sadie experienced anything like what she had with Ethan.

He was the man she'd looked for her whole life. And he was the one man she couldn't have.

Her heart broke a little even though her body was content, practically humming.

"That's good," Ethan said. "I really don't want you to move."

She laughed a little and turned her face into his chest. "We can't stay like this, Ethan. We'll starve."

"We can call out for pizza," he said. "I can reach the phone from here."

"And the delivery guy will bring it to us here?" She lifted her head and looked into his eyes. "A little embarrassing, don't you think?"

He grinned. "I'll toss the duvet over your excellent ass."

Her heart turned over in her chest. "Excellent? Thanks."

"Absolutely," he said, as he dropped one hand to her behind and squeezed. "Nobody sees that ass but me."

She thrilled to that and her too eager heart started celebrating. But she knew he didn't mean anything by it. He wasn't talking about permanence. Heck, he might not even really like her butt. It could all be the kind of things he said to every woman he took to bed. It would be foolish to build something out of nothing. And yet…

Sadie pushed those thoughts aside to examine later. For now, she kept her gaze fixed on his. "Your bed's a lot more comfortable than the desk."

She saw a flash in his green eyes and his hands on her butt tightened. "I've got a real fondness for that desk, now."

"Me, too," she admitted, then shivered.

"You cold?"

"A little," she said, then whooped when he rolled them over, covering her body with his.

"Better?"

"Better," she assured him, then gasped when he bent his head to taste one of her nipples again. "Okay," Sadie whispered, "not cold anymore."

He lifted his head to wink at her. "Glad to hear it. Now, let's get even warmer."

She swallowed hard, told her heart to slow down so it wouldn't simply explode out of her chest, and let herself slide into the feelings Ethan engendered in her. His hands were everywhere. He moved and she sighed. He touched and she moaned. He kissed and she hungered.

With her eyes closed, it was strictly a sensory world. She heard the bedside table drawer open again. Heard foil being ripped. Heard him sigh as he sheathed himself, and then he was turning her onto her belly, lifting her hips and pushing her legs apart. She turned her face to one side as she reached up to hold on to the padded, gray leather headboard. Then Sadie looked over her shoulder at him, saw him poised at her center and felt everything inside her melt into a puddle of need and love and desire so thick and heavy, her body ached with it.

How could she need him again so quickly?

She licked her lips and whispered, "Do it, Ethan. Take me."

His green eyes burned. His jaw was tight. Desire rippled off of his body in waves that washed over her and nearly took her under. Then he pushed himself home and she forgot everything.

She moved back into him, rocking, pushing. He ran his hands over her butt, then swept one down to touch her core as he drove into her from behind. Again and again, he was relentless, tireless. He pushed her, demanding she give him all she was, while he gave and took all at once. Their bodies slapped together and the heat in the room was breathless.

He was all. He was everything. What he could do to her. What she did to him. The magic they created together shone around them like fireworks raining down from the ceiling. He stroked her hard, pushing down on that tight, hard nub with his thumb, and Sadie shattered again. She screamed his name and only moments later, he shouted in triumph and emptied himself into her.

Bodies burning, hearts crashing, they curled up together, her back to his front, and dropped into exhausted sleep.

For Ethan, the next few days were…challenging. Not only did he have a new housekeeper and her five-year-old daughter living at the house, but he and Sadie had crossed the barriers separating them. She spent every night in his room, because what was the point of going in and out of the guest room?

Every night, they made love with a frantic fierceness that seemed to only get stronger. He couldn't stop touching her. Wanting her. He woke up in the middle of the night and reached for her. She'd become…essential. Ethan wasn't sure when that had happened or even *how* it had.

He'd wakened this morning to realize there were lotions and makeup lined up like tiny soldiers on his bathroom counter. In the shower, her shampoo sat beside his and made the whole damn room smell like lemons. Her clothes were in his closet, her shoes lined up alongside his, and when he'd finally noticed all this, he'd had one brief moment of panic.

It had been a long time since he'd shared any part of his home, his life, with a woman. And that had ended so badly, he'd promised himself he would never risk it again. But this was different, he assured himself. This situation with Sadie was temporary. This wasn't a mark of a relationship beginning, but of a business partnership ending.

"And I don't care for that, either." They still had almost three weeks on their deal and neither of them had spoken again about the fact that now that Julie was working for him, and willing to care for the baby, he didn't really need a nanny. At least, there wasn't a huge rush for one.

So why had he asked Sadie to stay? Why hadn't he told her that she could move out of his house?

"Because," he muttered, turning in his chair to stare out at the ocean, "you don't want her to leave."

Sure, it worried him to see how much she was settling into his home, his bedroom. But the nights with her were addictive. The more he had her, the more he wanted her. If she left, he might never get her back in his bed again, and Ethan wasn't ready to give that up yet.

And then there was Emma.

The tiny girl was carving out a place for herself in his heart and that was shocking, as well. He'd never expected to feel something for the baby. Care for her, sure. He owed Bill and his wife that. Ethan had made a promise and he intended to keep it. But he'd never been around kids much and he'd liked it that way.

Now Emma was opening his eyes to the idea that just maybe he'd been...wrong. It didn't happen often, which was why he hadn't recognized it right away. But he was a big enough man, he hoped, to admit when the unthinkable happened.

Only the night before, he'd been struck by just how

the changes in his life had affected him. He'd heard Emma stirring on the baby monitor and got up before Sadie could wake. In the dark, quiet house, he'd walked into Emma's room and crossed to the crib. The little girl opened her eyes, looked up at him and *smiled*. She knew him. Trusted him. Was happy to see him.

And in that instant, a bubble of warmth had spread through his chest and settled around his heart. He hadn't expected it, wasn't prepared for what it was going to mean to his life, but he also couldn't deny it.

Emma. Sadie. They were changing everything and it was quickly coming to the point where he couldn't remember what it had been like without them in his house. In his mind.

All he had left of his once orderly world was work. His company. And even that was under constant assault from Gabriel, though Ethan hadn't heard another word from his brother about changes. Which should worry him, he supposed. On the other hand, he'd take the break where he could.

Then a knock on the door sounded and Sadie poked her head inside. "Ethan. Ms. Gable from Child Services is here."

Well, that break didn't last long. He wondered if this was a routine check or if the woman had some idea of taking Emma from him. If that was her plan, she would be disappointed.

Emma and Sadie were his and Ethan wasn't ready to give either of them up.

Eight

"Send her in, Sadie."

Melissa Gable walked into his office with long, purposeful strides. Ethan silently gave her points for an intimidating presence. In her black suit jacket, starched white shirt and knee-length black skirt and sky-high heels, she looked all business. He supposed most people might wither and quietly panic beneath her steady stare. But Ethan wasn't worried. Ms. Gable wouldn't get anything he wasn't willing to give.

She carried a black bag the size of Montana on her left shoulder, and as he rose to greet her, Ms. Gable reached into the bag and pulled out a manila file folder.

They shook hands, then she took a seat opposite his desk. He sat down, too, studied her, waiting. He didn't wait long.

"I've already been to your day care here in the building to check in on Emma, see how she's doing."

"How did you know she wouldn't be at home with a nanny?" Just curious, he told himself.

"I didn't," she said. "But it's my job to be thorough, so I checked the day care first."

"And?" He offered nothing. He'd learned long ago that the secret to successful negotiations was remembering that he who speaks first loses power.

"She appears to be happy and healthy," Ms. Gable allowed. "And as a side note, I have to commend you on your in-house day care, as well. Unfortunately, there aren't enough employers farsighted enough to realize that a well-run day care is imperative in this day and age."

"Agreed." He nodded. "It pays to keep your employees happy, and when they don't have to worry about their kids, they're more productive." Well damn, that sounded cold even to him. Maybe that *was* why he'd begun the day care in the first place. But since Emma had arrived in his life, he'd realized just how important it was for people to be able to check on their children during the day. He'd been downstairs a few times himself.

"Yes. Well." She checked her notes, then looked at him again. "I've spoken to the day care operators, who tell me Emma is well fed, clean and obviously well cared for."

That irritated him beyond measure. "You expected she wouldn't be?"

"No, but even the most well-meaning people don't often pull things together as quickly as you seem to have." She flipped through to another page, scanned it, then said, "I went by your house earlier and your housekeeper showed me Emma's room. I approve of what you've done there and..." She checked again. "Julie, is it? She assured me that the baby is cared for and happy."

"Again," he said, tapping his fingers now against the desk. The desk where he and Sadie had taken each other for the very first time. Odd, but that stray thought eased the temper building within. "You're surprised?"

Ms. Gable closed the file, tucked it into her bag and said, "Forgive me, Mr. Hart, but you seemed less than happy when you discovered Emma had been left in your charge."

He winced internally at that, because she made a good point. He hadn't wanted the baby. Had resented that Bill had remembered that long-ago promise Ethan had made. But whether he'd wanted them to or not, things had changed. That baby girl had started out as nothing more than his responsibility. Now she was more. Now she was *his*.

Just then, he recalled Sadie telling him, "If you can't love Emma, maybe you should give her up to someone who can." And he thought about that. Thought about that tiny girl. How it felt when she curled her fingers around his. How *he* felt when she laid her head down on his shoulder. How right it was when he checked on her at night and saw her smile at him with delight.

He did love her.

Might not have wanted to. Might not have counted on this ever happening to him, but Emma was important to him now. And he'd give her up to no one.

"Mr. Hart?"

"Emma stays with me," he said flatly, coming out of his thoughts. "I'm looking for a nanny now and until I find one, my housekeeper, Julie, is helping us care for her."

"Us?"

"My assistant, Sadie Matthews, is assisting me with Emma, as well."

"I see." Nodding to herself, she stood up, held out her hand and waited for him to shake it. "Well then, from what I can see, you have this situation well in hand. I'll make my report to my superiors and recommend the guardianship become permanent. If you care to eventually legally adopt Emma, I'd be happy to help you in any way I can."

Surprised, but pleased, Ethan stood up and nodded. "I appreciate that."

Once the woman was gone, Sadie slipped into the room and closed the door, leaning back against it. "Well? What did she say? Do? Think?"

He laughed a little. Sadie's enthusiasm was contagious.

"Emma stays with me," he said.

"Really?" Sadie smiled at him and approval shone in her eyes. Strange how good it felt to know she was proud of him and what he'd done.

"I'm glad, Ethan."

"Why?" he asked, his gaze sliding over every square inch of her.

"Because I think Emma's good for you."

One eyebrow arched. "More direct honesty?"

Sadie shrugged. "A little late to change that now. Besides, would you prefer lies?"

"No," he said, his gaze locked on her. She was wearing what he'd always thought of as her "work uniform." Black slacks, dress shirt and short black jacket. And she looked sexier than any other woman would have in diaphanous lace or a skimpy bikini. Just looking at Sadie hit him on so many levels he couldn't have counted them all.

He wanted her.

As he did every moment of every damn day.

It didn't matter if she was laughing with him or her eyes were snapping with fury. Sadie Matthews was the one thing in Ethan's world he couldn't predict. Couldn't control. And he enjoyed knowing that more than he would have thought possible.

"It's not as scary as you thought, is it?"

Could she read his mind now?

"What's that?"

"Love."

The way she said that word sent a chill along his spine. He stiffened and his voice went deep and gruff as he demanded, "Who said anything about love?"

Her head tipped to one side, delighting him, even as her expression screamed disappointment. "I did. But you should. Ethan, you love that baby."

"I care for her, sure," he hedged. He wasn't going to use the *L* word because it didn't matter. He'd made Emma a part of his world, his life. He would take care of her, make sure she was happy. Wasn't that enough, for God's sake?

"Is it really beyond you to admit you know how to love?"

"It's not that I don't know how," he said tightly. "It's that I choose not to."

"And that's immeasurably sad."

He ground out, "Thanks so much."

"Ethan..." She took a step toward him and stopped. "I'll only be here a couple more weeks. When I leave, what then?"

A couple more weeks. Well hell, he didn't want to think about *that*. Time was moving too quickly. It wasn't only Emma who had invaded his life, it was Sadie, as well, and knowing she would be gone soon was like a thorn constantly jabbing at him. Ethan wanted to find a way to keep her with him; he just hadn't come up with anything yet. But damned if he'd lose Sadie now.

Marriage was, of course, out of the question. He'd

already failed spectacularly at that institution and he had no interest in repeating the mistake.

"You don't have to leave."

"We've been over this, Ethan."

"I don't want you to leave," he said abruptly.

"What?" She stared at him, shocked. "What are you saying?"

"I'm saying we're good together, Sadie." He came forward, took both her hands in his and held on tightly, stroking his thumbs across her knuckles. "We're a hell of a team. Why should we end it?"

"Ethan…" Her eyes shone and she licked her lips as if they'd gone suddenly dry.

"Things have changed between us, Sadie. You know it as well as I do. We have more together now." The thought of losing it was unacceptable. "You don't have to go, Sadie."

She looked as though she might be considering it, so he continued. "In the last couple of weeks, we've been more flexible with work time, right?"

"Work time." She frowned.

"Yes." He held her hands tighter when she tried to pull free. "You can work whatever hours you want. You can take your vacations and I won't call you out of family gatherings."

"I see…"

"And we can be together," he finished, pulling her up against him.

"Like we have been," she said softly.

"Exactly." He looked down into her eyes. "Sadie, the last couple of weeks have worked for both of us, haven't they?"

"Yes."

"So why change it?"

She gave him a small smile and shook her head. Ethan didn't like what he was reading in her eyes.

"Because I want more in my life than great sex and work," she said.

"What else is there?" Ethan demanded, though he knew damn well what her answer would be.

"*Love*, Ethan," she said, meeting his gaze with an intensity that almost slapped at him. "I want someone to love. I want to *be* loved. I want a family of my own."

"You have Emma," he countered, thinking of how close she'd become to the baby over the last couple weeks. "We both know you love that baby. I can see it whenever you hold her."

"I do. I really do. But she's not mine, Ethan," she said, shaking her head again. "She's a darling, but she's your baby. To her, I'll never be more than someone who comes and goes from her house. Like a visiting aunt."

"Then live there with us," he argued.

She took a breath, blew it out and said, "You want me to live with you, have sex with you, help you raise Emma and work here for you."

"Is that so bad?" The demand rolled from him in

deep, tight tones. "For God's sake, Sadie, we're doing all of that now. Why not keep doing it?"

"Because it's not enough."

"It is for me," he countered.

"Not for me." She swallowed hard and added, "If I'm going to have my own life, have what's important to me, I have to leave. To you, I'll never be more than your lover."

"And that's bad?" He released her hands and didn't let himself think how empty his hands felt.

"For me, yes," she said. "I need more, Ethan. I deserve more."

He couldn't argue with that, because she did deserve everything she wanted. But he couldn't give it to her. Wouldn't get married again.

"Fine." Nodding, he stepped back behind the desk, as if pulling on a suit of armor. "Well then, you'd better get busy finding your replacement here. And I'll still need a nanny for Emma."

"Ethan, I wish—"

He ignored that. "Get me marketing, will you? I want to have another look at the Mother's Day campaign before it's set in stone."

"All right."

"And bring me some coffee when you get a minute."

"Sure." Her heels tapped against the floor as she left the office.

When she was gone, he sat back in his chair and

told himself to get used to that empty sensation. It was going to be with him for a long time.

"You had sex."

"I did," Sadie said, and picked up the wine Gina had poured for her. "Many times."

"Finally." Gina sighed happily, took a sip of her own wine and demanded, "Who's the lucky guy?"

"Ethan."

Gina choked on her wine, slapped one hand to her own chest and coughed until her eyes ran. Feeling a little guilty, Sadie tried to help, but Gina shook her head and waved one hand at her. When she could finally breathe again, she cried, "What do you mean, many times? Are you crazy?"

Sadie had been asking herself that for almost two weeks now. And the answer was still the same. If she *was* crazy, she didn't care. "No. He's—"

"Don't. Don't even say it," Gina told her, and took a cautious sip of her wine. "Honey, I know I told you to have sex with him, but that was to get him out of your system, not to dig him in even deeper."

That's just what had happened, though. Even after the scene this afternoon at the office, Sadie couldn't regret what she'd had with Ethan. Yes, he'd made it plain that he wasn't interested in love. That he didn't want to give more than he had or risk more than he dared. And maybe she could understand why, even though she wanted to throttle him to make him see what they could have together if only he'd believe.

She'd left the office right after their…*meeting* and come to Gina's. Ethan was perfectly capable of driving Emma home and seeing that she had dinner. It would be good for him to do it himself. To see what it would be like without Sadie around to help. And oh, that thought broke her heart. She wouldn't be there to watch Emma grow up. Wouldn't be sleeping with Ethan. Or having sex with him. Or waking up snuggled next to him. She wouldn't even be working with him anymore, and boy, his absence in her life was going to leave a huge, gaping hole.

"I need cookies." Gina got up to rummage in a cupboard and came up with a bag of chocolate-covered marshmallow cookies. "This is my private stash. None of the kids know. Not even Mike has found them yet. But I'm willing to share with you."

"You're a saint." Sadie grinned and took a cookie for herself. Biting in, she took a quick look around. Gina's kitchen was bright and cheerful. White walls, red cupboards and black granite counters. There were sippy cups on the drain board and a row of baby bottles waiting to be filled. It was homey and cozy and light-years from Ethan's showplace kitchen. But, Sadie reminded herself, now that Julie was working at his house, she'd made some changes to the sterile atmosphere that could almost make it this warm.

"If I were a saint I wouldn't have told you to sleep with Ethan."

Sadie looked at her sister-in-law. "You couldn't have stopped me, either."

"Well, don't tell Mike that. I have him convinced I'm all powerful."

Sadie laughed and took another bite of cookie. "I can't help what I feel, Gina."

"But you're hoping this is going to turn into a fairy tale or something," the other woman said. "I can see it in your eyes."

"Well, that's annoying," Sadie admitted. Because of course that's what she'd been hoping for. Even knowing the chances of it happening were practically zip. And today had pretty much tied that up in a bow. Yet still, she hadn't completely given up. "Okay, yes, I'm hoping, but the more rational part of me knows this isn't going anywhere. But Gina, he's hitting most of the points on my list now."

"Really…" Gina ate another cookie and washed it down with wine.

Sadie ticked them off. "Sexy, oh yeah. Adventurous…" Thinking of the night before in the shower, she flushed with pleasure. "Boy howdy. He's spending time with me and he loves Emma."

"Has he actually said so?"

"No, but I can tell." He didn't want to say the word, but that didn't mean he wasn't feeling the emotion. The more time Ethan spent with the baby, the easier he was with her. Emma had wormed her way into the man's heart against his will and it was wonderful to watch. Whether Ethan knew it or not, he was opening up to the world. To possibilities. Why couldn't one of those possibilities be *her*?

"And sense of humor?"

"He has that, too," she insisted. "He doesn't show it often, but it's there."

"Sadie, that list was there to prove to you that Ethan wasn't the man for you. Instead, you're fiddling with it to make sure he meets all the criteria you have. That's not a good thing."

"I know." Restless, Sadie set her wine down and walked across the kitchen, picked up one of the baby's bottles and turned it in her hands. She wanted children of her own. A husband. A job she loved. Was that really too much to ask?

Not looking at Gina, she said, "We're still hunting for a nanny. When we find one, I'll go."

"I know you don't want to," Gina said.

"I really don't." Looking at her from across the room, Sadie gave her sister-in-law a sad smile. "I just love him. Like you love Mike."

"I know. But sweetie, setting yourself up for heartbreak isn't the smartest thing you've ever done."

"True. But honestly, if there is no happy ending here, at least I had this time with him."

"It won't be enough."

Sadie set the bottle down. "It'll have to be."

Gabriel watched as the chef made up the samples that they'd present to Ethan.

Making fine chocolates was more a science than

an art, though most people didn't realize it. Of course, there was plenty of art involved, as well.

Tempering the chocolate itself to the right temperature, where it would set up glossy and hard enough to *snap* when you bit into it. Mixing the ganache to the perfect texture before infusing it with the flavors Gabriel was hoping would convince Ethan to open his mind and try something new. Once the ganache was ready, the truffles and other assorted fillings had to be hand rolled into a uniform size and perfectly rounded or squared. Sometimes they used molds to get the right shapes, but here, in this rented kitchen, Jeff Garrett would be rolling the chocolates by hand.

As an assistant chef at Heart, Jeff was talented and eager to move up the ladder. Tonight was his chance at excellence, as well as Gabe's. Jeff already had the chocolates—milk, white and dark—tempered and waiting. The cold marble slab held rows of perfectly rounded truffles and ganache and were just waiting for Jeff to hand dip them and then stamp and decorate. Now that most of the basics were done, the chef as artist would take over. With talent and style, a good chocolate chef would make his creations shine like jewels.

"It smells great in here, doesn't it?" Gabe murmured, not wanting to disturb Jeff as he mixed the last of the spices into the final ganache.

"It does," Pam whispered, her gaze never leaving the chef and the chocolates laid out on the marble slab in front of him. "Do you still have the recipe with you?" she asked. "Just in case he has to start over, I mean."

"Don't even say it." Gabe shuddered and checked his watch. "Jeff's already been at it for hours. If we have to start over…"

"But the recipe's safe, right?"

He looked at her. "Yeah. Of course. Don't worry so much."

"I just…know how much this means to you, that's all." Pam watched as Jeff used a candy fork to hand dip a lavender truffle into the white chocolate melt. He carefully lifted it out, laid it on the cool marble, then swirled the chocolate on top by twisting the candy fork over it. He did the same with five more truffles until he had a tidy row laid out.

On another slab were pieces of what would be dark chocolate raspberry coconut bark drizzled with white chocolate.

Earl Grey tea truffles coated in cocoa powder were resting alongside white chocolate lemon blackberry bonbons. The last offering was a dark chocolate ganache infused with Sumatran coffee—Ethan's favorite—and orange liqueur.

The samples were flavorful and beautiful, as Jeff concentrated now on decorating each piece until it shone.

"The chef I was going to have you use would have made the bark white chocolate with dark chocolate drizzle. To showcase the red of the raspberry." Pam sniffed a little.

Gabe slanted her a puzzled look. "Jeff's creations look perfect."

"Oh, they're very nice." She shrugged. "I just think a more experienced chef might have done an even better job."

Okay, he thought, she'd been a little off ever since their first fight about the chef and she was still off tonight. Not really angry, but not herself, either. He'd wanted her there with him because it had really all started out as Pam's idea. The two of them together, facing down Ethan. But ever since Gabe had decided to use Jeff, Pam had been…different.

"What's going on with you, Pam?" Gabe asked. "Jeff studied with master chocolatiers in Belgium. He's been with Heart Chocolates for four years. He's worked his way up to being an assistant chef and he wants this almost as badly as I do."

"All true," she said with a shrug, "but you never even gave my guy a tryout."

"I didn't need to," he said, impatient now. After all, this might have started out as her idea, but this was his life. His company. She didn't have a horse in the race, so she had nothing to lose.

She flashed him a hard look and interrupted him. "I keep telling you, I thought we were in this together, Gabe. *We* were making decisions, and then suddenly, you changed the rules and I'm cut out. How do you think I should feel?"

He blew out a breath and tried to see it from her point of view. Gabe guessed he would have been pretty pissed if the tables were turned. But bottom line, this was his life. Not Pam's.

"I know you wanted to help," he said, striving for patience. He loved Pam, But damned if he understood her. "I do trust you. But this is my company. I've got to do what I think is best for it."

"I know, Gabe. Really. And I love you. I'm just..." she shrugged again. She shifted her gaze to Jeff.

Gabe watched as the man used an airbrush pencil to dazzle the white chocolate with rainbow colors in swirled patterns. As those colors began to set up, Jeff switched cartridges to paint a stylized red heart on top of the dark honey-infused caramels coated in a thick layer of milk chocolate.

"They all look great," Gabe said.

Jeff paused to glance up at him and smile. "Thanks, boss. The dark chocolate raspberry and chipotle chili are going to be coated in an extra layer of dark, then streaked with the milk in a heart pattern." He glanced around at his creations. "Then I think we'll be ready."

Ready to face down Ethan and demand he take a chance on the future. Hell, Gabe was betting everything on this as a win. Ethan's head would explode when he found out Gabe had taken the family recipe from the safe. So these chocolates had better damn well convince Ethan that Gabe was right, or working with his older brother from now on was going to be a living nightmare.

"When will you take these to Ethan?" Pam asked.

"Tomorrow," Gabe said firmly, nodding to himself. "You ready for it, Jeff?"

"So ready," the chef said, concentrating on the last of the chocolates he was creating. "I've got the boxes here. When they're finished setting up, I'll box them for tomorrow."

"In the morning. Be at my office at ten. With the chocolates. We'll face Ethan down together." He turned to Pam. "Are you going to be there?"

"Sure." She lifted her chin and met his gaze. "I told you before, Gabe. I'm with you."

Gabe dropped one arm around her shoulders. She was tense and stiff for a couple seconds, then she moved into him and leaned her head against his shoulder. He smiled to himself. Whatever was going on, they'd get past it. Once this was settled, he'd sit down with Pam and not let up until he found the answers he wanted. But for now, he had to focus on the plan he'd put everything into. He knew this was a step toward the future for Heart and damned if he wouldn't find a way to convince Ethan.

Gabe believed that. He had to. Because if he failed, he wouldn't lose only this chance at making a mark on the company. He might lose his brother.

Ethan was already in a crappy mood when Gabriel walked into his office the next morning. He hadn't slept all night because he hadn't had Sadie with him. For the first time since moving in with him, she'd slept in the guest room. Annoying to realize how much he'd come to count on having her there beside him.

She'd been right across the hall and yet she might as well have been hundreds of miles away. He knew what it would take to get her to come to him. And he couldn't give it to her.

Wouldn't, he corrected silently. She wanted a relationship. Something permanent. A family. A commitment.

Hell, he'd changed enough lately, hadn't he? He'd taken her into his house, into his bedroom. He'd been with her now longer than he had been with anyone else other than his ex. Ethan already knew he hadn't been a good husband. Why would he even *think* about trying that again? He liked Sadie. Liked being with her, so why would he risk making her miserable by marrying her? No. She might think he was being a selfish bastard by pulling away, but the truth was, he assured himself, he was doing this for her own good.

Let her find another man. His insides twisted at the thought. One who would hold her at night, make her belly swell with a child. He gritted his teeth and fisted both hands helplessly. Some other man would be the one to get her smiles, her kisses, her—

"Ethan," Gabriel said, splintering his thoughts, "we have to talk."

"Looks like more of a meeting than a conversation," Ethan observed. He looked from his younger brother to Sadie, to Jeff Garrett, one of their top chocolate chefs. A cold, suspicious feeling snaked along Ethan's spine and colored his tone when he demanded, "What's this about, Gabe?"

"Jeff and I have something we want you to try." Gabe motioned to the chef, who stepped up and set three small candy boxes on Ethan's desk.

His temper bubbled, but Ethan kept it tamped down. Gabe had done it. Gone behind his back and made up samples of the candies he wanted to incorporate into the company's product line.

Standing up behind his desk, Ethan looked at Sadie. "Did you know about this?"

"Nope," she said, and shot Gabe a hard look.

"Don't give Sadie a bad time. She didn't know a thing," Gabe said, and faced off against Ethan. Bracing his legs wide apart as if readying for a fight, he folded his arms across his chest and said, "This was my idea. Well, mine and Pam's."

He turned to hold out one hand toward a woman hovering near the doorway. "Come on in, honey. It's game time."

Ethan watched her walk to his brother and he frowned slightly. "Who's this?"

"Pam Cassini," Gabe said. "She's with me."

Amazing. He'd brought his new girlfriend in on this? Ethan studied the woman. She looked familiar somehow, but he couldn't put his finger on why. Frowning, Ethan set that niggling worry aside a second later because damned if he didn't have bigger issues at the moment.

Sadie walked up and stood beside him. Thankful for the support, he gave her a quick nod, then looked back to his brother.

Gabe was standing in a slash of sunlight pouring through the tinted windows at Ethan's back. He stood like a man waiting to hear a sentence pronounced. Well, he wouldn't have to wait long. "What the hell have you done?"

Nine

Gabe lifted his chin and met Ethan glare for glare. "I rented a professional kitchen and Jeff made up some samples of a few of the flavors I was talking to you about."

Ethan's gaze shifted to Jeff, who looked a lot more worried than Gabe did. As he should. "You know I could fire you for this," he said tightly.

Jeff swallowed hard. "Yes, sir, I know. But I agree with Gabe. It's time to push outside the box."

Astounded, feeling cornered, Ethan lifted his eyebrows. "In a box? You think Heart Chocolates is boring? Is that it?"

"No, he didn't say that," Gabe interrupted. "And

don't come down on him, either, Ethan. He can't fight back."

"But you can," Ethan said, and his voice was so controlled, so quiet, Gabe should have been wary. Instead, his brother looked defiant, rebellious. Situation normal as far as Gabe's attitude went.

Sadie caught Ethan's reaction, though, and silently slid her hand into his and gave it a squeeze. With that single touch, she dialed down his temper, his frustration, and helped him focus.

"What exactly did you do?" Ethan asked, and thought he was remaining remarkably calm, all things considered.

"I told you."

"Yes. But how did you make up the chocolate?" Ethan studied his brother. "For these 'samples' to be a true representation of Heart, you'd have to have access to the recipe."

The minute the words left his mouth, Ethan saw the truth on his brother's features. And his calm dissolved into a pit of white-hot fury. "You *took* the recipe?"

"I'm a Hart, too, Ethan," Gabriel argued, meeting fire with fire. "Yes, I took *our* recipe. I made a copy of the one in your safe."

Ethan actually saw red. That recipe never left the safe. It had been copied and protected and kept in a separate place, but the original... "How did you—"

Sadie tugged on his hand and he looked down at

her. "I ran into Pam and Gabe here in your office the night Emma arrived. I didn't mention it because I didn't think anything of it."

Could his head actually explode? Ethan stared into Sadie's big blue eyes and read a plea for patience. She was asking a lot. But for her, he'd try. He took a long, deep breath, glared at his brother and demanded, "What did you do with the original?"

"What do you think I did with it?" Gabe sounded offended now, which was astonishing to Ethan.

"How the hell do I know?" Ethan shouted, and when he heard himself he made a valiant effort to lower his voice. "I didn't think you'd take our heritage out of the safe and make a copy, so for all I know, you sold the original on eBay!"

"Don't be ridiculous." Gabe went to the safe, hit the dial lock, spun it a few times, then swung the door open. "There's the recipe. Right where it belongs. Do you really think I'd risk everything we are to prove a point?"

"Isn't that exactly what you did?" Ethan shouted again.

Sadie squeezed his hand once more, but this time he barely felt it. This was over the top. He felt betrayed by his own damn brother. He and Gabe had argued a lot over the years, but this was something he hadn't expected.

"Hell no!" Gabe went toe to toe with his brother, and met him glare for glare. "I used the recipe, but the chef involved already works for us. I trust him as you should, too, since he's one of our top guys."

Ethan gritted his teeth so hard he should have had a mouthful of powder. "Jeff isn't the issue here."

He heard the man's sigh of relief.

"Fine." Gabe threw both hands out in supplication. "I'm a traitor. Have me drawn and quartered tomorrow. But today, try the damn chocolates."

Stunned, Ethan could only stare at him. Gabe was still pretending this was no big deal. "Seriously? You expect me to go along with this when you went behind my back?"

"You didn't give me a choice, Ethan." Gabe pushed both hands through his hair, looked over at Pam, then back to his brother. "I wanted to do this with your approval. Hell, your involvement. But you're so damn stubborn. So resistant to change—"

"So really it's all my fault," Ethan said wryly.

"Well, I wouldn't have put it that way, but since you did…"

"You're something else, Gabe."

"Is it so hard to see my point of view, Ethan?" Gabe's voice was low and tight, filled with frustration that Ethan could sympathize with, since he was feeling it, too. "I'm not trying to wreck the company. I'm trying to make a difference and fighting you every damn day to do it."

"But you don't see it from my side, either. I don't want to change with the times," Ethan said. "Forever trying to figure out which way the wind's blowing in this business. It doesn't pay to chase trends."

"It doesn't pay to ignore advancements, either," Gabe argued.

"You guys..." Sadie tried to intervene, but neither of them acknowledged her.

"I'm not ignoring anything," Ethan said. "And I won't risk everything we are, either."

"I wanted him to use a chef I know," Pam said, speaking up for the first time. "But Gabe refused. He wouldn't risk that recipe. Instead, he insisted on using a Heart chef to protect it."

She still looked familiar to him and it was irritating to not be able to identify why. Still, she was emphasizing the point Gabe had made earlier. Mollified a bit, Ethan nodded and took a deep breath. He folded his hand around Sadie's and didn't even question why he was using her as a touchstone of sorts.

Gabe seemed to sense that the worst was over. He gave a signal to Jeff, who cautiously moved closer to the desk. Deftly, the man opened up the boxes, displaying the candies he'd personally created the night before.

"They're beautiful," Sadie whispered.

That they were, Ethan admitted silently. The variety of chocolates were artistically presented—everything from cocoa powder to the white chocolate bonbons decorated with a rainbow of colors.

"Thank you." Jeff grinned, pleased at the response.

"They're not just pretty," Gabe said, with satisfaction. "They're delicious."

Ethan scowled at him and Gabe grinned. "Admit it. You want to know what they taste like."

As angry as he was, Ethan also felt a ripple of pride in Gabe. He had his own vision and wasn't afraid to follow it. His brother had believed in something and found a way to make it happen. Not that stealing the family recipe was the way to do it, but Ethan admired that his brother believed in his own vision enough to risk everything.

"What if I don't like them?"

Gabe grinned even wider. "That won't be an issue."

"He seems sure of himself," Sadie said, with a wink for Gabe.

"Always has been," Ethan muttered.

Gabe walked to Pam and dropped one arm around her shoulders. He watched as Jeff laid out a white cloth napkin on the desk, then stepped back to wait. And watch.

"All right. Moment of truth." Ethan looked at Sadie. "I want you to try them, too. I trust your opinion."

She gave him a smile that lit up her eyes and Ethan's breath caught in his chest. Then he turned to the candy. He took one of the rainbow-decorated, glossy white chocolates.

"That's a lavender truffle," Jeff provided, then

looked at Sadie as she chose another piece. "And you have a dark chocolate raspberry coconut bark drizzled with white chocolate."

"Interesting," Ethan murmured, and carefully broke the white chocolate piece in half. Satisfied at the sharp snap of the chocolate coating, he then inhaled the scent, approving of the precise blend of spice and sweet. But the proof was in the flavor.

He bit into it and let the ganache melt on his tongue while flavor exploded in his mouth. He really hated that his brother had been right. The candy was perfect.

He shifted a look at his brother and saw the triumphant gleam in Gabe's eyes. "It's great, right?"

Chewing, Ethan nodded. "It is. Better than I would have thought."

Again, Jeff heaved a sigh of relief and Ethan couldn't really blame him. The chef had risked a hell of a lot, too. He'd worked his way up at Heart and he'd gambled his job on these samples.

"Sadie?"

She swallowed the bite she'd taken and shook her head in amazement. "This bark is terrific. The raspberry is sweet but not overpowering the chocolate, and the coconut gives it a slightly salty, savory flavor. Really amazing."

Jeff smiled and Gabe looked proud enough to burst. Ethan couldn't blame him. They went through the other chocolates one by one, with both Jeff and

Gabe explaining the process and how they'd chosen the different flavors they'd blended into the ganache.

"This last one is a Sumatran coffee, orange liqueur blend," Gabe said slyly.

"Clever," Ethan murmured. "Hit me with a flavor I love."

"I'll pass," Sadie said, and took one of the lemon blackberry bonbons instead.

Pam was strangely silent, but Ethan assumed it was because this wasn't really her business. She had nothing riding on this gathering; she was simply there to support Gabe.

"You did a hell of a job, here," Ethan ruefully admitted when the tasting was completed.

He'd been backed into a corner so neatly the only way out was Gabe's way. Ethan hated change, but he'd been dealing with nothing *but* change over the last couple weeks and it hadn't killed him. And really, the damn chocolate was *good*. Maybe Gabe had a point, after all, and it was time to branch out. To test new waters, before he—and his company—became so comfortable, neither of them could grow.

"That means what, exactly?" Gabe asked warily.

Ethan looked from the candy to Sadie to Gabe. "It means we should talk privately. Pam, would you and Jeff mind stepping out of the office for a few moments?"

"She doesn't have to go," Gabe argued.

"It's okay," Pam said with a weak smile. "I'll wait outside."

When they were gone, Ethan perched on the edge of his desk and said, "You made your point, Gabe. I don't like how you did it, but you were right about the candy."

Gabe clutched his heart. "Hold on a second. I might need an ambulance."

"Keep it up," Ethan promised with a quirk of a smile, "and you will."

Suddenly all business, Gabe asked, "So we'll go forward with the new line?"

"That depends," Ethan said, drawing Sadie over to his side and taking her hand in his.

Gabe's eyebrows lifted and a quick smile came and went. "Depends on what?"

"I don't want to start another line with only five or six offerings," Ethan said. "Can you and Jeff come up with a full dozen new flavors?"

"Oh, hell yes. Jeff's got a million ideas and—" He broke off. "You're making Jeff head chef on this project?"

"He earned it, don't you think?"

"I do. Between us, we'll come up with flavors that'll blow away the competition." Gabe was excited now, his eyes shining and a wide smile curving his mouth.

"Then go," Ethan said. "Be brilliant. But we decide together which flavors we're going to push."

"Agreed, Ethan. Thanks." Gabe went to pick up the candy boxes.

"Leave the candy," Ethan said, making his brother laugh.

Gabe walked out to tell Pam and Jeff the good news, leaving Ethan and Sadie alone in the office.

"That was well-done," Sadie said, and cupped his cheek to turn his face to hers.

"He pushes every button I've got, but he came up with some great new tastes, textures." Shaking his head, he sighed and said, "He went about it the wrong way, but I guess he was right about something else, too. I didn't really give him any other choice."

"Wow, self-realization," Sadie mused, smiling. "I think we're having a moment here."

He caught her hand in his again. "It happens."

"You didn't have to put him and Jeff in charge," she said. "That was well-done, too."

He gave her a quick smile. "Are you kidding? He wanted this new line—now he can be in charge of making it happen. Seems fair."

Sadie laughed. "So you give him what he wants and punish him for it all at once. You're devious."

"Yeah, I know." He pulled her in close. "I missed you last night."

"I missed you, too."

"I didn't want to," he said.

"I know." She smiled wistfully.

He looked into her eyes and found himself drowning in that deep, cool blue. "I can't be who you want me to be, Sadie. But do we have to leave each other before we leave each other?"

She tipped her head to one side, those blond curls of hers sliding across her skin. "No, Ethan. Let's be together while we can."

"Good call," he said, then he kissed her.

Gabe left the meeting ready to take on the world.

Hell, if he could convince Ethan to make changes to the company chocolate line, he could do anything. He expected to find Pam outside the office waiting for him, but he spotted her with Jeff by the elevators. And it looked like they were having a conversation spiked by hand gestures and angry expressions.

Frowning, he hurried toward them, ignoring the phones ringing, the clack of keyboards and the low, muttered conversations rising and falling all around him.

"I told you I can't do it," Jeff was telling Pam as Gabe walked up. "That's proprietary information."

Pam looked desperate, furious. "For God's sake, it's not like it's a secret. You saw it last night. I'm just asking you to tell me—"

"What's going on?" Gabe looked to Pam for the answer, but shifted his gaze to Jeff when the chef spoke.

"Pam wanted me to give her the Heart chocolate recipe."

"What?" Gabe looked at her, shocked. That made zero sense. She knew that recipe was the best-kept secret in the company. Hell, she'd just been present when his own brother had reamed him for copying it. "Why would you do that?"

She took a breath and blew it out. Her gaze shifted from side to side before finally meeting Gabe's. "Because I need it for my father's company."

"What the hell, Pam?" He kept his voice low, to prevent anyone else from listening in. Jeff slipped away and Gabe barely noticed. Suddenly, a lot of things were making sense. How eager Pam had been to make up those samples. How quickly she'd suggested using her own chef to make the candy. How furious she'd been when Gabe had used Jeff for the project instead of the chef she'd suggested.

God. He felt like an idiot for trusting her.

The elevator arrived with a loud ding and Pam turned for it, but Gabe grabbed her upper arm and held her in place. "You owe me, Pam. What the hell were you doing? Was any of this real to you? Was I just a means to the recipe?" He snorted a harsh laugh as reality crashed down onto his head. She'd never been into him. It was all about Heart chocolate. "Damn, I've got to admire you. You went all out for what you wanted. Pretending to love me just to make sure your plan worked. Must have been a bitch when I didn't use your guy."

She yanked her arm free and shot him a hard

look through flashing brown eyes. "Yes, it was hard. My brother's a chocolate chef. He could have made your candy and then kept the recipe for us to use against you."

Infuriated, confused, Gabe demanded, "Why? What have you got against the Hart family?"

The elevator started to close and she slapped one hand out to hold the doors open. "Because my last name isn't Cassini, Gabe. It's *Donatello*."

"What?" Everything Gabe thought he knew went right out the window. Stunned, he thought back to all the times he'd discussed business with her. How he'd told her about the Donatello buyout and how his brother was eager to take over the shop in Laguna and introduce a new venue for Heart Chocolates.

Hell, he'd *trusted* her.

Gabe looked at her as if seeing her for the first time. And still he didn't know who he was looking at. The woman he loved? Or an industrial spy? "You lied to me this whole time?"

"It wasn't all a lie," she countered, voice breaking as the first tears filled her eyes. "Cassini is my mother's maiden name."

"Oh, well then. That's okay." Shaking his head, Gabe fought down the fury clawing at his throat as he looked at the woman he loved. The woman he'd thought was with him. A partner. "Are you even really in PR?"

"No. I make chocolate. With my family. Just like you."

"Of course you do," he muttered thickly. No wonder she'd known so much about the chocolate industry. "And you wanted to ruin Heart Chocolates as what? Payback for us buying your father out?"

"Your brother is ruining my father's life," she said, her voice urgent, desperate. "Dad can't stand up against a company the size of Heart. He has no choice, he *has* to sell because the great and powerful Ethan has decided he needs a street location and he's focused on my dad's." A hot rush of tears spilled from her eyes and streamed down her cheeks unchecked. "The Donatellos have been running that shop for forty-five years, Gabe. It's just as important to us as your company is to you. My brother and I grew up in that shop. It means everything to us."

Her tears shook him to the bone. He wanted to reach out to hold her, tell her everything would be okay, but he wasn't sure it would be. Hell, he didn't even know what he was feeling at the moment.

He loved Pam Cassini. But did that woman even really exist?

"I do love you, Gabe," she confessed. "I didn't mean to, but I do. I wasn't pretending about that. But this is about my *father*. I had to do whatever I could to help." She jumped into the elevator and kept her gaze on him as the doors slid shut. "I love you…"

"Damn it, Pam…" He lunged for her, but the doors shut him out. Then she was gone.

* * *

A few hours later, Sadie sat in the front passenger seat of Ethan's car while Gabe leaned forward from the back, still talking. They'd *been* talking for hours. Ever since Pam had dropped her bomb on Gabe.

"It's her father, Ethan," he was saying, not for the first time. "We can understand family loyalty."

"Agreed," Ethan said, giving his brother a quick look before shifting his gaze back to Pacific Coast Highway. He was just as shocked as Gabe by Pam's revelation. But at least now he knew why the woman had seemed so familiar. Ethan had met personally with Richard Donatello, and his daughter resembled him quite a bit. "She went about all of this the wrong way, but at least you two have something in common."

Sadie said, "Ethan, that's not really fair. Yes, Pam lied, and okay, I guess Gabe did, too..."

"Hey."

"Well, it's true," she said, and patted his hand. "But you both had good reasons for it."

That was surely true. From the moment he'd charged back into the office to tell Ethan exactly who Pam Cassini really was, Gabe had been like a man possessed. He couldn't stop talking about the woman. Ethan glanced at Sadie and didn't miss her wistful expression. Was she envious of what Gabe felt for Pam?

"I didn't expect you to take it this well," Gabe

admitted. "I thought you'd be supremely pissed that Pam had used me to get to the recipe."

"I have to admit, I'm with Gabe. You surprised me, too, Ethan." Sadie was watching him, and even with his gaze on the road, Ethan felt the power of her stare.

He understood why the people closest to him were shocked at his reaction. As little as a month ago, he'd have been furious, with Gabe *and* Pam. But it was impossible to be too angry with Gabe when Ethan himself had been allowing his emotions to guide his actions the past couple weeks.

"Let's just say that there have been a lot of changes lately and maybe I'm still responding to them." Ethan shot her a quick look and saw the smile that curved her mouth. "I'm not happy," he admitted, "but I can understand what she did."

He made a turn onto a side street in Laguna and pulled up outside a Craftsman-style bungalow. The house had a big tree out front, a wide porch boasting twin rockers and a small table between them. The winter flowers in the pot by the front door were a cheerful spot of color on a gray day. He turned off the engine and half turned to look at Gabe. "That's why we're here. I want to talk to Pam's father—her family—about this."

"Right." Gabe scraped one hand across his jaw. "What did he say when you called?"

"Richard already knew before I could tell him.

Apparently," Ethan said, "she'd confessed the whole thing to her parents when she left you at the office. Richard's eager to talk it all out."

"That's good, right?" Gabe scrambled out of the car and stood in the street, staring at the house as if he could see past the walls to the woman he loved.

Ethan climbed out, too, and looked at his brother. He hoped this was going to end well, but he didn't have a clue what would happen when both families talked. As Sadie got out of the car, Ethan's gaze naturally drifted to her. It felt good to have her with him. Too good, really, because he was depending on her now even more than he had when she was simply his assistant. But that was a problem for later.

Ethan took Sadie's hand and she held on, glad that he automatically reached for her. She wondered if he even realized how often he did it. And she wondered how she would get along without his casual touch.

Richard Donatello opened the door for them and welcomed them inside. His daughter looked a lot like him, which was why Ethan had thought Pam seemed familiar, Sadie figured. The house itself was cozy and a lot bigger than it looked from the outside.

Richard led them through the house to the dining room, where his wife, son and Pam were waiting for them.

"Thanks for seeing us," Ethan said.

"No problem. Please. Sit." Richard took the chair

at the head of the table and waited until they were seated before speaking. "Thanks for not having Pam arrested."

"Dad!"

"You could have been," her father said, his features stern.

The woman winced and gave Gabe a furtive look.

"This is my wife, Marianna, and my son, Tony." Richard paused and said sadly, "Pam told me what's been going on and I'm offering you my apology."

"Dad—" Pam interrupted, but her father shut her down with a single look.

Sadie sympathized. She knew Pam loved Gabe. And she could guess at how Pam had felt, torn between two loyalties. But of course she'd stood for her family. What wouldn't a person do for family?

"Your apology isn't necessary," Ethan said, and gave Sadie's hand a squeeze. "My brother and I were just saying that if there's one thing we understand, it's family loyalty."

"Thank you." Richard nodded, then looked at Gabe before turning to his daughter. "You were wrong to do it, Pam. And Tony, you shouldn't have gone along."

His son nodded. "Yeah, I know, Pop. We were only trying to help," he said. "To save the shop."

Sadie watched the people around the table, waiting to see where this would go. There was tension in the room, but over it all were threads of love so thick and interwoven she half expected to actually *see* them, like golden strands linking the Donatello family together.

"This isn't a hostile takeover," Ethan put in, but before he could say more, Pam interrupted.

"Of course it is. You're Heart Chocolates. Donatello's doesn't stand a chance in a fight against you."

"Pam," her mother said softly. "It's not a fight. Ethan came to us a couple of months ago with an offer to buy the shop. We talked about it—" she sent her husband a smile "—and after more negotiations, we decided together to accept."

"But why?" Pam asked, looking from one parent to the other. "Because you couldn't afford to fight back. That's why I wanted the recipe. I thought maybe we could barter for it. They get it back and we keep the shop."

"So blackmail?" Richard asked, dumbfounded. "You would do something like that?"

"To help the family, yes. I'm not proud of it, Dad," she said, and looked straight at Gabe. "I didn't want to. Didn't want to lie. But I didn't know how else to help you save the business."

"We don't want the shop," her father said, loudly enough to get everyone's attention.

Sadie was startled by that and it appeared everyone but Ethan was, too. Silence dropped onto the table in the wake of that announcement until Richard's son spoke.

"What do you mean?" Tony asked, obviously stunned. "It's ours. We've been working it together my whole life."

"And enough's enough," their mother said, smiling at her husband.

"I'm confused," Gabe muttered.

"You're not alone," Pam said, and gave him a sheepish smile.

Sadie squeezed Ethan's hand in solidarity. He looked at her and smiled, apparently knowing exactly where the rest of this story was going. He leaned in closer and said, "Remember when you suggested I talk to Richard myself instead of sending the lawyers?"

"Yes..."

"Well, I did." He winked at her and Sadie was more confused than ever. "Just listen," he said, and they both turned back to the others gathered around the table.

"I'm retiring," Richard said, letting his gaze slide around the table. "Your mom and I want to do a little living while we still can."

"But you're not old enough to retire!" Pam was clearly shocked.

"That's what makes it even better," Marianna said with a smile for her husband. "Why wait until we need someone to push us around in wheelchairs? No.

We want to enjoy ourselves, Pam. It's past time for your dad to stop working so hard."

Richard nodded, smiling at his family. "Your mother's right."

"But the shop…" Pam simply stared at her father.

Richard shrugged that aside. "It's been good for us. Made us a decent living. Put you two through school and I enjoyed it, too. We both did. Working together, side by side, to build something special."

Marianna and her husband shared a secret smile that Sadie envied. This couple had what she dreamed of having. A real partnership. They'd worked and lived and loved together for decades.

"With the money Heart Chocolates is paying us for the location and our customer list and website, well…" Richard winked at his wife. "I can take your mother on all the trips she's wanted to take for years. We're going on a cruise, in May. First-class. To Europe. For our thirtieth anniversary."

"Europe?" Tony was astonished.

Sadie sighed at the romance of it all. How wonderful must it be to still love so fiercely that you wanted *more* time together, even after all those years.

"That's right," his mother said with a bright smile. "We're going to have some fun for a change. And stay up late every night, since your dad won't have to get up at three o'clock in the morning…"

"Looking forward to that," Richard said, grinning at Ethan.

"So this was all for nothing," Pam whispered.

This was such a private moment, if not for Ethan's tight grip on her hand Sadie would have felt like an intruder. But for now, anyway, she and Ethan were united. He wanted her there and that meant everything to her.

"I feel like an idiot." Pam looked at Gabe. "I'm so sorry. I didn't mean to betray you. Or lie to you."

"I know," he said, pushing up from his chair to walk around the table and pull her to her feet. "I love you, Pam Cassini Donatello."

She gave him a watery smile and leaned into his chest, sighing when his arms came around her. "I love you, too, Gabe."

"Isn't that lovely?" her mother said. "Maybe we'll get a wedding to plan, too."

"Mom!" Mortified, Pam turned her face into Gabe's chest as he laughed.

Ethan shook his head at his younger brother and Sadie could almost hear him thinking *Not love, Gabe. Anything but that.* And her heart hurt as she realized there was no happy ending in this story for her. She and Ethan would part ways and all she'd have were the memories she'd made over the last weeks. That sounded unbearably sad.

Ethan turned to Richard. "So the deal's still in place? No more negotiating?"

"It better be in place," Marianna said. "I just made reservations for the cruise today."

"We have a deal," Richard said, and held out one hand. "I know better than to disappoint my wife. But if you don't mind my saying, you should hire my son, Tony, there. He's a hell of a chocolate chef."

"Dad!"

"Done," Ethan promised, as the two men shook hands.

A half hour later, Ethan and Sadie left the house together. Gabe stayed with Pam and Sadie had a feeling that Marianna was going to get the wedding she was hoping for. Sadie felt a pang of envy she tried to bury. Just because she wouldn't end up with her hero didn't mean she couldn't be happy for someone else.

"I'm glad that all worked out," she said, as Ethan held the car door open for her.

"Yeah." Ethan glanced back at the house. "Me, too. Gabe's in love. Never thought I'd see that."

Sadie took a breath and held it. She could let this go, but what would be the point? "It can happen to anyone, Ethan."

He looked down at her and shook his head slowly. "No, it can't. What you and I have is different, Sadie. I don't want to hurt you."

God, she felt cold. "Then don't."

Pulling her into the circle of his arms, Ethan held her close for a long minute. Sadie inhaled the scent of him, wrapping it around her like a cloak. She held on to him, luxuriating in his strength, his warmth, for as long as she could, because she felt like this was already a goodbye. He was letting go of what they had. Even if she wasn't leaving yet, a part of Ethan already had.

When he stepped back suddenly, his eyes were shadowed, like a forest in twilight. "Sadie, it's not that easy."

"I wonder why you're looking for the easy way, Ethan," she said softly. "Nothing worth having comes easy."

She couldn't keep looking into his eyes, watching as the shutters came down and the walls went up. So she slid into the car and he slammed the door after her. A couple seconds later he was in the driver's seat, turning to fix a hard stare on her.

"I'm not looking for easy. None of this is easy." It was a demand that she understand, and she'd heard that tone so many times over the last five years, Sadie didn't even blink in the face of it.

"It is," she said flatly, and watched a flash burst in his eyes. "It's much easier to walk away than to stay and work for what you want."

"I'm doing this for you," he said, clearly angry and just as obviously trying to control it.

"Doing what, Ethan? Turning away? Shutting me out? Thanks, but I didn't ask you to."

"You didn't have to," he countered. "You think I don't see what's happening between us? What you're hoping for? I already know I make lousy husband material, Sadie. I made Marcy miserable. I don't want that for you."

Under her breath, a short, sharp laugh escaped her. "And it's all about you, is that it?"

"In this, yes." He snapped his seat belt, fired up the engine and pulled away from the curb with a squeal of tires. "You should be thanking me," he muttered.

"Right." Sadie turned in her seat and glared at him. "I should thank you for breaking my heart."

"Damn it, don't you get it yet? That's what I'm trying to avoid."

"Well you're too late," she snapped. "See, I already love you, you idiot."

Ten

Ethan swung the car to the side of the road, turned the engine off and said tightly, "Don't. Just... Don't."

"You don't tell me what to do, Ethan," Sadie said. "FYI."

"Damn it, Sadie. What're you thinking? I didn't want you to love me."

"You don't get a vote in everything," she said, shaking her head in complete amazement. Of course this was how he would take being told she loved him. Most men might feel a little surge of panic and then be happy about it. But not the man *she* loved. Oh, no. He fought like a caged wolverine.

"This is exactly what I was trying to avoid with

you, Sadie." His voice was so low, she almost missed the words, and she really wished she had.

"Contrary to your own belief system, Ethan, you don't actually control the universe."

He turned his head to look at her. "You're making jokes about this?"

"Would you rather I cry?"

"God, no."

"Then laugh it up. I intend to." Eventually. At the moment it was taking everything she had not to give in to the tightness in her chest, the burning in her eyes. But damned if she'd cry in front of him. That really would be a cherry on top of the humiliation sundae.

"Really." It wasn't a question, but that's how she took it.

"Yes, Ethan." Sadie tipped her head to one side to stare at him. "I'm going to laugh at the absurdity of me loving a man for five years and he never noticed."

"Five…" His shocked expression would have been funny if it hadn't been so damn sad.

"Or how about the fun of telling that man I love him and having him order me to stop."

"Sadie—"

"I'm going to laugh because it's ridiculous." Her heart hurt, but damned if she'd let him see it. Whatever tears she would shed, she'd cry them in private. And maybe she wouldn't cry at all.

She'd known going in that loving Ethan was futile. She hadn't been able to help herself, so she was

willing to accept the pain that was the inevitable re-
sult of being a damn fool. Sadie had seen today that
it wasn't *all* Hart men who were incapable of loving.
Just the one she wanted. And maybe it was time she
simply accepted that and moved on.

"Look, Ethan, we've already agreed that I'll be
leaving when we find the right nanny." She took a
deep breath. "So let's just find her fast and pretend
we didn't have this humiliating conversation, okay?"

"Damn it, Sadie…"

"Seriously, Ethan," Sadie said, giving him a hard,
steady look. "I'm so done with this. I don't want to
hear you're sorry or you're angry or whatever, okay?
These are *my* feelings and I don't need you to tell me
what to do with them."

"Fine." His jaw was tight and his green eyes were
on fire, so situation normal.

"Good." She turned in her seat, faced the front
and said, "Now, let's get back to the house. I want
to see Emma."

That tiny girl wouldn't be in her life much longer.
As hard as it was, Sadie was going to make finding a nanny her top priority. She couldn't stay with
Ethan now that he knew she loved him. Because the
one thing she *never* wanted from Ethan was his pity.

She loved him.

Ethan felt twin jolts of differing emotions—both
pleasure and panic, with a little guilt tossed in. He

shrugged his shoulders, trying to drop the burden. Hell, he hadn't asked her to love him. This wasn't his fault. Yes, she was wounded now and that pained him more than he wanted to admit. But her pain was far less than she would have felt if he'd tried to make a relationship work.

Ethan nodded, silently reassuring himself that he was doing the right thing as he stared out the office window at the steely sea. Sunlight pierced the clouds and slashed at the surface of the water like a golden sword. And the beauty of it all should have been enough to clear his head. But it wasn't.

It had been two days since her confession. Two days since they'd solved the Gabe and Pam problem, only to fall into one of their own. They'd lived like polite strangers ever since and the tension in the house was so thick Ethan could hardly breathe.

Emma was the only bright spot in his life and he didn't miss the irony in that. The baby girl was the reason all of this had happened to his once orderly life in the first place, and now that everything was turned upside down, it was Emma alone who could make him smile.

He'd interviewed four nannies in the last two days and Ethan felt the pressure to find someone fast. The sooner he did, the sooner Sadie could leave and they could try to get past this mess.

Sadie. Leaving. It was the right thing, but it didn't feel that way.

A knock at the office door had him turning. "Yes?"

Sadie stepped inside and Ethan's heart gave a hard jolt in his chest. He ignored it. That was hormones. Lust. He hadn't touched her in days and his body missed hers. Hell, the sex had been great, so why wouldn't he react to her? It had nothing to do with her big blue eyes. Or the way she sang to Emma first thing in the morning. Or how she smelled. Tasted. The sound of her laugh, the touch of her skin.

"What is it, Sadie?" He sounded gruff even to himself.

One of her blond eyebrows arched. "Rick's taking over for me this afternoon. I'm going to the house to get Emma. Take her to a doctor appointment."

He straightened at that. "What's wrong with her?"

"Nothing, Ethan," she said, tipping her head to one side, and he knew she was doing it on purpose now. "She needs a checkup."

His heartbeat settled down as he nodded. "All right. Can Rick handle your desk?"

She lifted her chin. "I've been working with him. He can do the job if you're patient with him at first."

Since Ethan and Gabe weren't at war any longer, there'd been no reason why Rick from Marketing couldn't take over for Sadie. He wasn't as good at it as she was, but then no one would be.

"I'm not going to slow walk him, Sadie," Ethan grumbled. "If he can't do the job find someone else."

"He can do it, Ethan. Just don't be a jerk and you won't scare him into paralysis."

Shaking his head, he said, "Still feeling free to say whatever you're thinking, huh?"

"Freer than ever," she said with a sharp nod. "I've got to go."

She left and Ethan was alone again. Damn it.

They found the nanny that afternoon.

The woman was impeccably qualified and Sadie was trying very hard not to resent her for it. Teresa Collins was perfect. Her résumé. Her references. She'd been trained at a world renowned nanny academy, for heaven's sake, and Emma had taken to her instantly. Not to mention that at forty plus, Teresa wouldn't be leaving to start a family of her own. In other words, the woman was everything they'd been looking for.

Standing out in the backyard, where she could be alone and think, Sadie noted the finished fence— four feet of terra-cotta-colored brick topped by another two feet of wrought iron. Emma would be safe, she told herself. And happy.

She'd grow up in this beautiful house with Julie and her daughter, with a perfect nanny and with Ethan. The only one missing would be Sadie. And since she was so young, Emma would never know that someone else had loved her, too.

Instead, the nanny would get all Emma's smiles

and hear her first words and see her first steps. At that thought, Sadie had to wonder if Ethan would stay involved with the baby. Would he back away and leave it all to the nanny because it was easier?

This was Sadie's own fault, of course. She never should have stayed the extra time. Never should have moved in here with Ethan and absolutely shouldn't have had sex with him. But that part was really hard to regret. In fact, the only thing she was sorry for was that he hadn't touched her in days.

Not since the night she'd told him she loved him and he'd reacted like a vampire to a rope of garlic.

"Sadie?"

Speak of the vampire... She turned from the ocean view to watch Ethan walk toward her, and her heart did a spin and jolt just looking at him. She really needed to go. Soon. For her own sake.

"What're you doing out here?" he asked, when he was close enough.

"Just looking at the fence." She glanced at it again. "They did a nice job."

"Yeah. The view's screwed, but the baby will be safe."

Shaking her head at that, she faced him and scooped windblown hair from her face. "What did you want, Ethan?"

"I've given Teresa the bedroom beside Emma's so she'll be close."

"That's good."

"And I asked Julie to pack your things."

She sucked in a gulp of ocean-scented air and swallowed the knot of pain lodged at the base of her throat. "Well, that's…abrupt." But not surprising. Looking into his green eyes now, she didn't see the slightest hint of the man she'd spent the last nearly three weeks with. Ethan had tucked that man away and maybe he'd never escape again. He was back to being the all-powerful, distant CEO. The man who never let emotion touch him. And it was clear to Sadie that he'd already said goodbye to her and what they'd shared.

"It's best this way."

"Your way, you mean," she said softly. "The easy way."

He tucked his hands into his slacks pockets and his expression went blank, giving away nothing of what he was feeling, thinking. "The deal was you'd stay until we found a nanny. Well, Teresa's here now, so—"

"Time to get things back to normal, is that it?" Well, she'd planned on leaving today, anyway.

"It is." His jaw was tight, the only signal to her that he wasn't completely at ease with this. Funny how it was such a small thing that could ease what she was feeling.

"You're right, Ethan. It's time for me to go."

He nodded, clearly relieved, and she laughed shortly.

"What's so funny?"

"This whole situation. I've loved you for a long time, Ethan."

He winced at the words and she couldn't help the sharp jab of pain in her heart. But she ignored it to say what she had to say. "I know you and I know you're going to try to hide from Emma like you've been hiding from me."

Scowling, he insisted, "I haven't been hiding."

She held up one hand for silence, because she wanted to finish this before she did something ridiculous and cried. "Yes, you have, but that's not what I'm worried about."

"You don't have to worry about me." The wind tossed his hair across his forehead and somehow that simple thing made him seem more approachable. More vulnerable.

"I probably will, anyway, but that's my problem, not yours." God, just looking at him made her want to cry for what they could have had together. "What I want you to do is promise me that you won't ignore Emma."

"Why would I—"

"Because it'll be easier," she said, and she knew he was remembering when they'd talked about taking the easy way before. So was she. "Easier to turn her over to Teresa and tell yourself it's better that way. But it's not, Ethan. Don't cheat Emma, and more importantly, don't cheat yourself."

"Sadie…"

She shook her head. She didn't want to hear whatever he might say, because she was certain it wouldn't be what she most wanted to hear. That he loved her. That he needed her. That he didn't care about past failures and he wanted only her.

"Good luck, Ethan," she said, and started walking. Sadie really hoped that Julie had finished packing her clothes because she needed to get out of there fast—before her heart convinced her to stay and fight for what she wanted.

For the next week, Sadie slept in late, painted the living room in her condo, bought new plants to kill and visited her nephews and new baby niece. She drank with Gina, cried on Gina's shoulder, then came home to her empty place and told herself that it would get better.

Soon, she hoped.

Because sleeping was almost impossible. She worked in her garden, moved furniture around and played with her nephews, all in an effort to exhaust herself, and still she didn't sleep. How could she when her bed was as empty as her heart?

"Okay, this is enough already," Gina said, pouring another glass of wine for each of them.

Sadie took a sip and looked through the sliding glass door to where her brother was shrouded in thick smoke from the barbecue. His sons were on the trampoline and with every jump, the springs shrieked.

"Agreed," Sadie said, chuckling as Mike waved an oven mitt, trying to dissipate the smoke. "I say we go out for tacos."

"I'm not talking about Mike's latest attempt to be Gordon Ramsay," Gina told her. "I'm talking about you and the pouting fest."

Sadie sniffed in insult. "I don't pout. I sulk. It's much classier."

"Well sure, but I'm tired of it, so I'm doing something about it."

Sadie took a sip of wine, shot her sister-in-law a sidelong glance and asked, "What did you do?"

"I fixed you up with Josh. The firefighter on Mike's squad that I told you about?"

"Right." Sadie did remember talking about the possibilities there, but how could she be interested in someone else when her mind and heart were focused on Ethan?

"You're going to meet him for coffee tomorrow afternoon."

Dread settled in her stomach. This was not a good sign. She was in no shape for a date. She hadn't slept. She had bags under her eyes deep enough to pack for a month-long vacation and she wasn't finished sulking. "Oh, Gina, I don't think so."

Gina scowled at her. "Sadie, you've been...*sulking*—"

"Thank you."

"—for more than a week now. You're in love with Ethan, but you're not doing anything about it."

Shocked, she demanded, "What can I do?"

"I don't know, fight for what you want?"

Hadn't she said something like that to Ethan not so long ago?

"I thought you were anti-Ethan," Sadie said.

Gina waved that off. "I'm anti-you-being-hurt. But if you love him, fight for him."

Shaking her head, Sadie said, "If you can't win, what's the point in fighting?"

"If you give up before you start, what's the point of anything?" Gina stopped and said, "Sorry, sorry. I told Mike I wouldn't butt in."

"Fat chance of that," Mike shouted from outside.

"Ears like a bat," Gina muttered, then said louder, "Here's the deal. If you're not going to fight for Ethan, then it's time you let yourself see that there are a few million other men out there. I told Josh you'd meet him at CJ's Diner in Seal Beach for coffee tomorrow afternoon."

Why did everyone think they could order her around? "Did you tell him what to order for me?"

"Sure," she said. "Coffee. Weren't you listening?"

Sadie laughed. She couldn't help herself. Gina was a force of nature. "Fine. What time am I meeting him?"

"Four," Gina said. "I told him if coffee goes well, you'll have time to get dinner."

"There, or are we going somewhere else?"

"Oh, I'll leave that up to you two."

"Hah! She gave Josh a list of restaurants!" Mike

shouted, and slammed the barbecue lid down, trying to smother the flames erupting from the grate.

"Just suggestions," Gina shouted back.

"I appreciate it, Gina," Sadie said, and it was true. It was nice to be loved so much. Her family was her rock. Knowing that Mike and Gina had her back made what she was going through more bearable. But in spite of her good intentions, Gina couldn't know just how far out of "dating" mode Sadie really was. "But—"

"Don't say no, sweetie." Gina leaned in and squeezed Sadie's hand. "Just give Josh a chance. Meet him for coffee. See what happens. What could it hurt?"

Ethan was fine.

No problems here. He could concentrate on work again now that his world was back in order. He didn't have the distraction of Sadie to keep him from concentrating. It was only the memory of her that haunted him now. He sensed her all over his house. Her scent lingered on the pillow she used. Her shampoo was still in his shower—he should toss it out, but he hadn't. He heard the phantom echo of her laughter and when he closed his eyes, he saw *hers*.

And the office wasn't much better. Hell, he could hardly stand to sit at his desk because of the memory they'd made *there*. Plus, as much as he tried to focus, he kept half expecting Sadie to briskly knock on his office door and poke her head inside. Instead, it was Rick manning the desk outside his office, and he wasn't nearly as good at the job as Sadie had been. In the man's defense, though, nobody would be.

Hell, two days ago, they'd lost an entire shipment of chocolates when a train derailed in Denver. Sadie would have had the whole situation taken care of in an hour. This time, it was Ethan himself who'd had to handle the crisis because Rick was out of his depth.

It was only natural that Ethan would miss her, wasn't it? She had kept his life, his office, running smoothly for five years, so it only made sense that her absence would throw everything off-kilter.

"And just who're you trying to lie to?" he muttered, and tossed his pen onto the desk. "It's not Sadie's efficiency you're missing. It's everything else about her."

"Talking to yourself is never a good sign."

Scowling, Ethan looked up at Gabe. "It's traditional to *knock* before you come into a room."

"I'm a rebel," Gabe said affably as he crossed the room and dropped into the chair opposite Ethan. "So, I'm here to let you know Jeff's come up with several more candies we'll have ready for you in another week or so."

"Good." Ethan picked up his pen again and pretended to read the papers in front of him. "Great. Goodbye."

Gabe laughed. "Nice talking to you, too. You

know, you used to be easier to get along with. Wonder why that was. Oh. Maybe it was Sadie's influence."

"You want to stop talking now." Ethan lifted his gaze and gave his brother a hard glare.

"No, I don't."

Ethan tossed the pen down again. "Damn it, Gabe, this is none of your business."

Gabe shrugged. "Yeah, but you helped me out when the Pam situation got so screwed up. Thought I'd return the favor."

"I don't need help." And even if he did, he wouldn't ask for it. He'd been fine before that insanity with Sadie and he'd be fine again. At some point.

"Pam and I are engaged."

Surprising, but not. Ethan was happy for his brother, but he really didn't want to hear about love or marriage. Didn't want anything else to remind him of Sadie. "Congratulations. Get out."

Gabe laughed and settled in for a chat. Irritated, Ethan wondered what it would take to get rid of him. Probably dynamite.

"Pam's brother, Tony, has been working with Jeff on the new line."

"I know."

"He's as good as Richard said he was. Of course, Jeff's still in charge, but Tony's really pulling his weight." Nodding, Gabe added, "And we've contracted for the rehab on the Donatello shop."

"I know that, too." They'd agreed to use Donatello's storefront in Laguna to launch their new line. Gabe and Pam were in charge and Tony and Jeff would be the chefs. It would be a good test spot and if it worked, which Ethan was sure it would, they'd think about opening up more specialty stores. He wanted to tell Sadie all about it. Hear her thoughts, ideas and suggestions. She had a sharp mind and wasn't afraid to give her opinion, and damn it, he missed that, too.

"I saw Sadie yesterday."

Ethan's head snapped up and Gabe grinned. "Got your attention with that one, didn't I?"

Yeah, he had. It felt like years since Ethan had seen her. "How is she?"

"She's doing great. Looked happy. She was out with her sister-in-law, shopping at Bella Terra. You know, the Huntington Beach mall."

"I know what it is," Ethan grumbled. So Sadie was out shopping and having fun and probably dating. Why wouldn't she? Who would she be going out with? It wasn't as if she'd had a lot of time to meet anyone. Or had she already met this mystery man before she left Ethan's life? How? When? Most importantly, *who*?

The thought of her with another man was enough to send ice through Ethan's veins. But he'd let her go, right? So he'd just have to live with that decision.

How did Sadie think that walking away was easy?

Nothing about this was easy.

"When are you going to admit you miss her?"

"When are you going to butt out of my life?"

"When you stop making a mess of it." Gabe leaned forward. "Sadie's not Marcy."

Ethan drew in a deep breath and settled the blast of anger he felt at Gabe throwing his past at him. He was right, though. Sadie was nothing like Marcy. Sadie would stand up and tell him what she was thinking. Marcy had kept her resentments to herself. Hadn't told him that she was unhappy. Not that their marriage's failure was her fault. He hadn't put the time in and he knew it. What he realized now was that a woman like Sadie wouldn't have put up with him ignoring her.

But Sadie wasn't the problem, was she? It was *him.* Ethan was the same man who'd made a mess of his marriage, so how could he know this time would be different?

"And you're not the same, either," Gabe said, as if reading Ethan's thoughts. "Sadie changed you."

Change. Used to be Ethan hated that word. Now, he could almost see the good in it. He had changed. For the better?

How was he to know?

"I'm just saying," Gabe added, as he stood up, "you might want to try to fix this before the chance gets away from you."

"I think it's too late already," Ethan murmured, remembering the look on Sadie's face before she'd left his house. Not only had he let her go, he'd practically shoved her out the door. Why would she be willing to walk back in?

"Yeah," Gabe said, "but you won't know until you try."

Eleven

Josh was nice.

At any other point in her life, Sadie would have really enjoyed him. The man was gorgeous, seriously built, and he had a great smile and a wonderful sense of humor. In short, he was everything she should have wanted. Sadly, the one thing he was not was *Ethan*.

Sitting across from him at the diner, Sadie listened while he talked about the fire station and the guys he worked with. But instead of *hearing* him, she was thinking of Ethan. Wondering what he was doing. How he was feeling. Did he miss her or was he counting his blessings to be rid of her? God, that was a horrible thought.

"Hey," Josh said, distracting her. "Are you okay?"

"I'm sorry," she said quickly. "Yes, I'm fine. I'm just…tired, I think."

Sunlight slanted through the window and lay across the bright red Formica tabletop. Just across the street was the ocean, shining in the winter sun, and the crowds on Pacific Coast Highway belied the winter cold. Nothing stopped Californians from enjoying the beach.

Sadie just wished she was in the mood to enjoy *anything*. Maybe Gina was right, she told herself. Maybe she'd done enough sulking. How long could she mourn a love that hadn't happened? Was she going to wither up and spend her life sulking? Wind up alone with a houseful of cats? The best way to forget a particular man was in seeing another one, right? Well, Josh was a good place to start. She didn't even like cats.

"We can do this another day," he said with a shrug.

"No, really. I'm okay." She shrugged off her dark thoughts, pushed Ethan completely out of her mind and focused on the man opposite her. "And I'm interested. Tell me why you decided to become a firefighter."

He grinned. "It's always dangerous asking a man to talk about himself. We could go on for hours."

Sadie laughed. "I'll risk it."

Josh started talking then, and this time she really

tried to pay attention. But less than a minute later, Ethan walked into the diner, carrying Emma against his chest, and Sadie was lost.

Following her shocked gaze, Josh looked over his shoulder, then back to her. "What's going on? You look like you've seen a ghost or something."

"Or something," she said, wondering what was going on. Her heartbeat was racing and her mouth was dry. Her stomach did a quick spin and flip, and she had to fight to keep her coffee down.

Ethan strode up to their table and completely ignored Josh as he said, "Honey, don't do this."

"What?" Sadie blurted.

"I know we've had some problems," Ethan continued, as if she hadn't spoken. "But we have a *baby*. You can't just walk away. We need you."

Horrified and embarrassed, Sadie stared up at Ethan. She couldn't believe he was doing this. And how had he found her? Groaning internally, she thought *Gina*. It was the only way. But *why* was he doing this?

"What's going on?" Josh gave Sadie a hard look. "Who is this? Gina didn't say anything about you having a baby. Or a husband."

"He doesn't know about us?" Ethan looked wounded as he stared down at her. "Even if you're mad at me, you can't forget about our child. Sadie, we need you. Come back home."

"Oh, for heaven's sake." She snapped a furious

look at Ethan, then shifted her gaze to Josh. "This isn't what it looks like." She choked out a strained laugh. "Really. That's not my baby—"

And right on cue, Emma crowed in delight and threw herself at Sadie. Defeated, Sadie instinctively caught her and cuddled her close. She was warm and soft and smelled so good, Sadie smiled while the baby patted her cheeks with both tiny hands. Oh, how she'd missed this baby.

"Okay," Josh said, "I don't know what's going on here, but I'm out." He slid off the bench seat, tossed a ten dollar bill on the table and said, "Good luck with whatever this is."

When he left, Sadie looked up at Ethan and scowled at the wide grin on his face. "Why would you do that, Ethan?"

He shrugged amiably. "I needed to get rid of him and I was afraid you wouldn't let me." He dropped onto the seat opposite her.

"Well, you're right. I wouldn't have." Sadie tried to be angry, but it was hard, with Emma cuddling in as if she were right where she belonged. "Gina told you where to find me, I'm guessing?"

"Not without telling me exactly what she thought of me first," he admitted. "The woman has a creative vocabulary."

Sadie laughed helplessly. Of course Gina would tell him off and then lead him right to Sadie. Beyond all else, her sister-in-law was a hopeless romantic.

The waitress came up with a fresh cup and poured coffee for Ethan, then refilled Sadie's. She left with questions in her eyes and Sadie couldn't blame her. She had plenty of questions herself.

"Why are you here?" she asked, keeping her voice down. "Why did you bring Emma?"

"When you're going to fight, bring all of your ammunition," he said, and Sadie was more confused than ever.

"Fight for what? What do you mean?"

"It means I want you to come back."

His gaze met hers. Sadie held her breath. "Come back to what?"

"To work."

She let the breath out and felt disappointment wash over her in a wave so heavy it weighed her down. "No."

"I thought you'd say that," Ethan said, cupping both hands around the mug of coffee. "So I'm offering you twice your old salary."

Sadie's heart sank even further. The minute she'd seen him, her foolish heart had hoped that he was there to confess his love. To ask her to marry him. To live and love with him. But he only wanted her back at the office and that, she couldn't do.

"No. I don't want to work for you anymore, Ethan." She scooted off the bench seat, snatching up her purse as she moved. It was hard to give Emma back to Ethan, but she did it, in spite of the fact that the baby reached up both arms to her and screwed up her tiny face to cry. "If that's why you came, you wasted a trip."

"It's not why." He stood up, too, tossed another ten on the table and led her out of the diner. "Not completely. Come on. We're not doing this here."

"Doing what?" She came to a dead stop on the sidewalk and refused to be budged until she knew what he was up to. Traffic hummed past, the wind howled in off the ocean and she had to squint up at him because of the sun.

He glanced around and frowned at the crowds and the noise before turning back to Sadie. "This isn't the place I would have picked, but screw it. This needs saying."

Sadie couldn't take much more. Tears were threatening and her throat was so tight she could hardly breathe. She had no idea what he wanted now, but she wished he'd just get it over with so she could go home. She had more sulking to do.

"Hold the baby," he said, and held her out so Sadie's only choice was to take the tiny girl.

"Okay, I offered you double your salary and you said no."

"I did," she said, "so don't throw more money at me."

"What if I offered you something else instead?"

She sighed heavily and smoothed Emma's wispy hair back from her forehead. "Like what?"

"A side job." He reached into his pocket, pulled out a blue velvet ring box and flipped it open.

She went perfectly still. Sadie was nearly blinded by the sun glancing off the enormous diamond nestled inside. Her heart actually stopped before it jumped into a wild gallop she had no hope of easing. She looked from the ring up to him and saw light and passion and love shining so brightly in his eyes it almost dimmed that diamond's gleam.

"Marry me, Sadie," he said, and the world seemed to suddenly fade away.

She couldn't hear the traffic or the people around her; all she could hear was the man she loved saying the words she'd never thought to hear him say.

"I know I'm not a good bet," he said. "And I admit, I was too scared to tell you how I felt because I didn't want to make another mistake. But I do love you. I love you so much it's making me crazy not being with you."

Sadie took a deep breath and held it. Emma leaned her head on Sadie's shoulder as if she was watching the show and cared about the outcome.

"I realized something last night, Sadie. The only mistake I was making was in *not* marrying you. You make me laugh. You make me think. You made it impossible for me to live without you. You made me love you."

"Oh, Ethan…" Tears filled her eyes and she blinked frantically to clear her vision.

"I can say the words now," Ethan told her. "I should have said it before. But if you say yes, I'll tell you how much I love you every day until you're sick of hearing it."

"That would never happen," she whispered.

His eyes speared into hers, and it was as if he was willing her to see inside him to the truth shining there. "Marry me and take your old job back, too."

She laughed wildly.

"Seriously. Come back to work, too." He grinned at her. "That way I can kiss my assistant anytime I want to. And you'll save me from Rick. He's terrible."

Still laughing, Sadie shook her head and tossed her hair out of her eyes. She didn't want to miss a moment of this.

"Marry me, Sadie," he said. "I fired Teresa."

Surprised, she held Emma a little tighter. "What? Why? She was perfect."

"No she wasn't," he said. "She wasn't you. I only needed a nanny because I was going to be alone with Emma. If we're married we can take care of Emma and all of our other kids together. And Julie's there to help, right?"

"Right…" Together. *All of our other kids.*

"If we're married—"

"Stop," she said, and stepped into his arms. She didn't need to hear anything else. He'd already said everything that mattered. Everything she'd dreamed of hearing for so long.

When he held her, pulling her tight and close, Sadie's heart started beating again. His warmth enfolded both her and Emma, and Sadie knew that this was the absolute best moment of her life.

"Is that a yes?" he asked, smoothing her hair back and out of her eyes.

"It's a yes. To everything." Sadie went up on her toes and kissed him. "Oh, Ethan, I want you and Emma and more kids, and my job."

"Thank God."

"It won't be easy," she teased, as he slid that diamond onto her ring finger.

"Who wants easy?" He scooped Emma up, then dropped one arm around Sadie's shoulders, turning to walk toward the parking lot. "You know, when we tell our kids about how Daddy proposed, we're going to have to come up with a more romantic story."

"Oh no, we don't," she said, leaning into him as they walked through the crowded streets. "This was perfect."

He kissed the top of her head and said, "I swear I'll be a good husband and father."

"I know you will," Sadie said, smiling up at him. "Because I'll be with you every step of the way."

* * * * *

#2641 LONE STAR REUNION
Texas Cattleman's Club: Bachelor Auction
by Joss Wood

From feuding families, rancher Daniel Clayton and Alexis Slade have been star-crossed lovers for years. But now the stakes are higher—Alexis ended it even though she's pregnant! When they're stranded together in paradise, it may be their last chance to finally make things right...

#2642 SEDUCTION ON HIS TERMS
Billionaires and Babies • by Sarah M. Anderson

Aloof, rich, gorgeous—that's Dr. Robert Wyatt. The only person he connects with is bartender Jeannie Kaufman. But when Jeannie leaves her job to care for her infant niece, he'll offer her everything she wants just to bring her back into his life...except for his heart.

#2643 BEST FRIENDS, SECRET LOVERS
The Bachelor Pact • by Jessica Lemmon

Flynn Parker and Sabrina Douglas are best friends, coworkers and temporary roommates. He's becoming the hardened businessman he never wanted to be, but her plans to run interference did *not* include an accidental kiss that ignites the heat that has simmered between them for years...

#2644 THE SECRET TWIN
Alaskan Oil Barons • by Catherine Mann

When CEO Ward Benally catches back-from-the-dead Breanna Steele snooping, he'll do anything to protect the company—even convince her to play the role of his girlfriend. But when the sparks between them are real, will she end up in his bed...and in his heart?

#2645 REVENGE WITH BENEFITS
Sweet Tea and Scandal • by Cat Schield

Zoe Alston is ready to make good on her revenge pact, but wealthy Charleston businessman Ryan Dailey defies everything she once believed about him. As their chemistry heats up the sultry Southern nights, will her secrets destroy the most unexpected alliance of all?

#2646 A CONVENIENT SCANDAL
Plunder Cove • by Kimberley Troutte

When critic Jeff Harper's career implodes due to scandal, he does what he vowed never to do—return to Plunder Cove. There, he'll have his family's new hotel—*if* he marries for stability...and avoids the temptation of the gorgeous chef vying to be his hotel's next star.

Get 4 FREE REWARDS!

We'll send you 2 FREE Books plus 2 FREE Mystery Gifts.

Harlequin® Desire books feature heroes who have it all: wealth, status, incredible good looks... everything but the right woman.

FREE Value Over **$20**

They'd never talked about how they were always overlapping
each other with dating other people.

It was an odd thing to notice.

Why had Sabrina noticed?

Sabrina Douglas was his best girl friend. Girl, space,
friend. But Flynn felt a definite stir in his gut.

For the first time in his life, sex wasn't off the table for
him and Sabrina.

Which meant he needed his head examined.

After the tasting, Sabrina chattered about her favorite
cheeses and how she couldn't believe they didn't serve wine
at the tour.

"What kind of establishment doesn't offer you wine with
cheese?" she exclaimed as they strolled down the boardwalk.
Which gave him a great view of her ass—another part of her
he'd noticed before, but not like he was noticing now.

Not helping matters was the fact that he didn't have to wonder what kind of underwear she wore beneath that tight denim. He knew.

They'd been friends and comfortable around each other for long enough that no amount of trying to forget would erase the image of her wearing a black thong that perfectly split those cheeks into two biteable orbs.

"What do you think?" She spun and faced him, the wind kicking her hair forward, a few strands sticking to her lip gloss. He reached her in two steps. Before he thought it through, he swept those strands away, ran his fingers down her cheek and tipped her chin, his head a riot of bad ideas.

With a deep swallow, he called up ironclad Parker willpower and stopped touching his best friend. "I think you're right."

His voice was as rough as gravel.

"You're distracted. Are you thinking about work?"

"Yes," he lied through his teeth.

"You're going to have to let it go at some point. Give in to the urge." She drew out the word *urge*, perfectly pursing her lips and leaning forward with a playful twinkle in her eyes that would tempt any mortal man to sin.

And since Flynn was nothing less than mortal, he palmed the back of her head and pressed his mouth to hers.

Don't miss what happens next!
Best Friends, Secret Lovers *by Jessica Lemmon,*
part of her Bachelor Pact series!

Available February 2019 wherever
Harlequin® Desire books and ebooks are sold.

www.Harlequin.com

Want to give in to temptation with
steamy tales of irresistible desire?

Check out **Harlequin® Presents®,
Harlequin® Desire** and
Harlequin® Kimani™ Romance books!

New books available every month!

CONNECT WITH US AT:

Facebook.com/groups/HarlequinConnection

 Facebook.com/HarlequinBooks

 Twitter.com/HarlequinBooks

 Instagram.com/HarlequinBooks

 Pinterest.com/HarlequinBooks

ReaderService.com

**ROMANCE WHEN
YOU NEED IT**

PGENRE2018

Love Harlequin romance?

DISCOVER.

Be the first to find out about promotions, news and exclusive content!

Facebook.com/HarlequinBooks

Twitter.com/HarlequinBooks

Instagram.com/HarlequinBooks

Pinterest.com/HarlequinBooks

ReaderService.com

EXPLORE.

Sign up for the Harlequin e-newsletter and download a free book from any series at **TryHarlequin.com.**

CONNECT.

Join our Harlequin community to share your thoughts and connect with other romance readers!
Facebook.com/groups/HarlequinConnection

HARLEQUIN®

**ROMANCE WHEN
YOU NEED IT**

Earn points on your purchase of new Harlequin books from participating retailers.

Turn your points into **FREE BOOKS** of your choice!

Join for FREE today at
www.HarlequinMyRewards.com.

Harlequin My Rewards is a free program (no fees) without any commitments or obligations.

YOU HAVE JUST READ A HARLEQUIN® DESIRE BOOK.

Discover more sensual stories starring **powerful heroes**, **scandalous secrets**...and **burning desires**. Be sure to look for all six Harlequin Desire books every month.